Katy,
book ...
dhm forever grateful!
Judy Hogan
8-4-12

Killer Frost

by

Judy Hogan

Mainly Murder Press, LLC
PO Box 290586
Wethersfield, CT 06129-0586
www.MainlyMurderPress.com

Mainly Murder Press

Copy Editor: Paula Knudson
Executive Editor: Judith K. Ivie
Cover Designer: Karen A. Phillips

All rights reserved

Copyright © 2012 by Judy Hogan
Paperback ISBN 978-0-9836823-8-7
Ebook ISBN 978-0-9846666-5-2

Published 2012 in the United States of America

Mainly Murder Press
PO Box 290586
Wethersfield, CT 06129-0586
www.MainlyMurderPress.com

Dedication

For Margie Ellison,
with whom I worked to make things better in Chatham
County and who taught me so much about love and egged
us all on to speak our truth

Acknowledgments

I am deeply grateful to Suzanne Flandreau, who has faithfully read my mysteries since 2007, and her suggestions have improved my books. Two Malice Domestic judges gave me hope: Katy Moore, who selected me as a finalist in 2011, and Ellen Rininger, who gave me good comments in 2008 and believed I'd one day be on bookshelves everywhere. Sisters in Crime, and the Guppies, in particular, helped me learn the publishing world, and on Guppy Press Quest I learned about Mainly Murder Press. Our outstanding Press Quest leaders, Diane Vallere and Kendal Flaum, encouraged me. Many other people have believed in my writing and cheered me on over the years, including Louise Penny, Julia Spencer-Fleming, and Kaye Barley. Two close friends here, Elaine Goolsby and Gene Dillard, have been especially supportive, and there are others, too. Thank you to all.

One

Tuesday, February 13, 2001. It was a love that came upon her out of the blue, which she knew she would never understand or be able to explain to anyone else, not even to Oscar and especially not to her husband. As calm and rational as Kenneth had been for the eight years of their marriage, he couldn't or didn't want to understand why she cared so much about Oscar, and she never had told him the whole story. She knew she was lucky to have Kenneth in her life, but her love for Oscar had been like a lightning bolt out of a cloudless sky, one of those connections you accept finally without understanding them.

It began when their dear friend Rick Clegg, Pastor of Ebenezer Baptist in Riverdell and a long-time activist, called them in Wales in early February and told Penny there was an interesting teaching job open for the rest of the 2001 spring semester. His friend from grad school, Oscar Ferrell, was the new Chairman of English at St. Francis, a black college in Raleigh. Oscar had fired a part-time teacher, and he needed someone right away to take her place. Could Penny and Kenneth come back to Riverdell two weeks early so she could teach part-time for him? With her experience teaching composition and creative writing at Orange Community College, this HBCU (Historically Black College or University) would be a piece of cake and pay better, too. He talked her into it, and Kenneth was game, too. They changed their air tickets and in twenty-four hours were on their way to North Carolina.

~

Once Oscar had seen her résumé and spent half an hour with her, he hired her before she'd handed in her official application. They had arrived in North Carolina on Saturday, and he hired her Monday. Her first classes were on Tuesday.

Oscar was waiting for her in his office at 7:45 a.m., and they walked together down the hall to Classroom 402. "Are you nervous?" he asked.

"A little," she admitted. She set her bag on the floor beside the desk (battered heavy oak but functional), took out her notes, the sign-up sheet, and the seating chart she had prepared. Classes had begun January 10, and it was February 13. She knew she needed to learn their names as fast as possible. She'd had students at the community college try to fool her. "Oh, I was here, Ms. Weaver," when she'd marked them absent. Then some African Americans had experienced white people not being able to tell them apart. She could and would.

Oscar said, "Jane Avery, the teacher I had to fire, was so lethargic as to be inert, plus she was incompetent. Don't assume they've learned anything. Do what you can in the nine weeks left in this semester. Maybe you can get some of them through this Pre-Comp course so they can move into Freshman Composition next term."

"I hope so," Penny said. The room they were in was square, as large as two normal living rooms, and the walls were a discolored cream color. Various styles of student desks, from old wooden ones, scarred with pencil and knife marks, to shiny new molded black plastic with chrome legs, were in no visible order. Maybe the last class had broken into groups? After consulting her, Oscar began arranging them in rows while Penny wrote her name and telephone number on the board.

She had just written down the homework assignment for February 15 when the first student walked in. He had to walk around his muscles. Penny had never seen anyone look so bloated. He wore jeans that had slipped to ride around his hips, revealing his red and white striped boxer shorts. Was he showing off the St. Francis colors? The muscles across his upper arms and chest (were those his pecs?) were huge. He had rolled back his tee shirt, the better to show them off. He walked slowly, awkwardly, not looking at her, and headed for the seat farthest away from her in the back row by the window. Then, once he'd worked himself into a chair, he stared out the window. It was as if she didn't exist. She glanced at Oscar, who turned and walked over to the young man.

"Good morning. I'm Professor Farrell, Chairman of the English Department. May I know your name?" Oscar was polite, down to earth, but his voice commanded attention.

The young muscle man looked at Oscar, who was slight, smiled, then glanced out the window again as if whatever he saw there was far more interesting. Then he turned back. He looked at Penny while he said, "It's Ronny. Ronny Glover. She our new teacher? I heard Miz Avery quit."

"Yes, Ronny, you'll have Ms. Weaver for the rest of the term. Where are you from?"

"Camden, New Jersey."

Oscar nodded. "We'll get started in a few minutes." They all looked toward the door where a young woman had entered. She was heavy-set, soft-looking, with long, straightened hair resting on her shoulders. She didn't look at Penny or Oscar but turned sharply when she reached the next to last row of chairs and walked toward Ronny, choosing the last seat, next to him, in the back row.

"Good morning," Oscar said, turning to the young woman. "May I have your name?"

"Merilee Taylor," she said softly.

While Oscar drew out Merilee, Penny finished writing down the homework assignment. Other students were drifting in. Oscar had said she had twenty-five students in this class—too many for a comp class, but he had only recently gotten the Provost's permission to lower the maximum enrollment to twenty for the following fall semester. He had taken over the English Department the previous August.

Penny glanced at her cheap Casio special. 8:05. There were about twelve students who had taken seats. Where were the others? She began passing around the roll sheet, which asked for campus contact info, and then a seating chart. She explained it to the young woman who had just scooted in and was sitting in the front row next to the door. "This is the seating chart I'll use so I can learn your names more quickly. Look at it upside down. This is the front row here. If you like this seat, write your name here, and then pass it around. I'm Ms. Weaver, by the way, your new teacher."

The young woman nodded, looked Penny over, and without smiling, took the chart and wrote "Lashandra

Steele" in the square that represented her seat. Then she looked up at Penny, tossed her dreads, which were carefully braided and bright with colored beads, and smiled. She handed the paper to the girl sitting behind her. Penny smiled back as Oscar walked to the front of the room and said to the whole class, "Good morning."

He got their attention instantly. They quieted, then echoed his greeting. I'll have to remember and use that ritual, Penny thought. It has a calming effect on them, and on me, too. Oscar waited while two more students hurried in at nearly ten after. There were still about ten students missing. "Close the door, please, Terence," Oscar said to the last young man who'd glided in. When he smiled at Oscar and returned to get the door, she saw that most of his teeth had gold caps. His dreads had not been combed recently. They looked matted and shopworn. What was the term? Nappy. He had an air of unconcern, like he couldn't be bothered with what any teacher or person in authority thought. He was insouciant. That was it. Oscar must know him. He was staring at him.

Terence grinned slyly at Penny as he eased his lanky body, well over six feet, into the black plastic chair next to Lashandra.

"Class, as some of you know ..." He gave Terence a hard look. "... I'm Professor Farrell, the Chairman of the English Department here at St. Francis. I'm here today to introduce your new instructor for English 21, Ms. Weaver. She'll be with you until the end of the spring term. Ms. Avery has left us."

Terence raised his hand. "Why?" he asked before Oscar could recognize him.

Oscar gave him a hard stare and didn't answer. "Ms. Weaver has been teaching composition at Orange Community College. She'll be of great help to you in passing this course, which is a non-college credit course. When you pass it, you'll be able to enroll in English 30 next term, the regular Freshman English course, for credit. The placement test you took when you enrolled placed you in English 21. That means you have a lot of basics to master, and if you do your part, I'm confident you'll be able to move quickly to English 30. Any questions?"

Lashandra raised her hand. "Do we still turn in our assignments from when we had Ms. Avery?"

Oscar turned to Penny, who nodded. "Yes," he went on, "and I expect you all to work hard to catch up to where you need to be as entering freshmen." He looked again at Terence, who was whispering to Lashandra. "Now please give Ms. Weaver your full attention." Oscar took a seat in the front row, to the far left of Penny, and smiled at her. She stepped over to stand in front of her desk. "I'm very happy to be here at St. Francis. I live in Shagbark County, in Riverdell, about forty miles from here. I've always heard good things about St. Francis. I'm also a poet. I'll be teaching a Creative Writing seminar this term, too. I've written my email and home telephone number on the board in case you need to reach me. I have no phone on campus."

She glanced at Oscar, who was frowning. "My office hours will be 11:15 to 12:00 on Tuesday and Thursday, after that Creative Writing class, in the Writing Center, which is in room 406 right around the corner. I'll also usually be there after this class until the seminar at 10:00. Because I'm part-time, I don't have an office, and I'll only be on campus Tuesdays and Thursdays from 8:00 to 12:00."

At this point the door opened, and three more students, all boys, came in, looked nervously around, and walked to the back of the room, where they slid down into their seats as if they wished to be invisible and grinned covertly at each other. They were all heavy and muscular but nothing like Ronny. Their muscles didn't look like balloons. Football players?

Oscar glared at them, got up, walked across the room behind Penny, and turned the lock on the door, then stood with his back to it, watching the students, not unlike a cat, ready to pounce if a mouse dared show its whiskers.

He's not sure I'm up to these kids, thought Penny. I'm not sure I'm tough enough either. There had been people who had tried and failed to manipulate her over the years. Not only landlords and her ex-husband, but all her children had given it a try when they were not much younger than these freshmen. She would have her challenges, but she was maybe more comfortable in the black community than Oscar realized. The kids clearly would try to work her, this Terence, for one. So she would have to demonstrate her authority as their teacher. She didn't look forward to it. She told herself it was like all the other hard things she had done in her life. Why was it she was always taking on hard, if not impossible, things?

She looked at the students, some whispering to their neighbors, others waiting patiently for her to continue, Terence staring at his desk. He had no book bag, no pencil or paper. Lashandra, next to him, was watching him when he wasn't looking, then glancing at Penny.

When they realized she was waiting for them, the students stopped whispering. "I've told you a little about me. Now I'd like you each to tell me a little about you. Take two or three minutes and tell me your name, your major, where you're from, and how you feel about being here at St. Francis. I understand that this is your first year, and for some your first semester."

The first three or four students gave quiet, unexceptional answers. But when Oscar slipped out the door, everything changed. It was the turn of a girl sitting in the back row. "My name is Sheila Green. I'm a Drama major from Petersburg." She paused, glanced around. "I hate St. Francis so far. The dorms have roaches, the bathrooms are nasty, the food makes me puke."

Penny saw the smirks on the faces of the girls around her. The football boys, as she would come to think of them, laughed but stopped when Penny looked at them.

Sheila had more to say. She looked very happy as she said, "I have to go to the restroom. May I be excused now?"

Then Lashandra, who had already introduced herself, raised her hand.

"Yes?"

"Can we leave now? The class ends at 9:00, and Miz Avery always let us go early."

Penny glanced at her watch. It was 8:30. "No, Lashandra. This class ends at 9:15."

"No, it don't." Lashandra had a mulish look.

"Miz Avery allus left us time to get us our breakfast. She never kept us till 9," chimed in Sheila.

Penny reacted blindly before she took time to think. "Sheila and Lashandra, I'm not Ms. Avery. We have only seventy-five minutes together twice a week. I will dismiss class at 9:15. You can use the restroom at 9:15. Now, who's next?" She nodded to the plump young woman sitting next to Ronny and deliberately didn't look at Sheila or Lashandra.

"My name is Merilee Taylor." Penny could barely hear her and had forgotten her name. She moved down the aisle toward her. "I'm from Camden. My major is Music. I like St. Francis okay."

Penny looked at her seating chart to be sure she had the name right. "Thank you, Merilee. Now, Ronny?"

Ronny turned away from his window but looked across the room toward Terence on the front row as he said, "I'm Ronny Glover. I'm from Camden, too. I'm here to play football. I just want to walk across the stage and get my certificate. This the third college I been at. It's okay here. I just hope I ain't kicked out again." He was serious, but there were giggles around the room. When Penny looked around, they stopped.

Several more students commented on their frustrations with the college: bad food, "nasty" dorms. Terence, the tall one with gold teeth, waved his hand until she called on him. "Our dorm is the pits. The bathrooms are stinky, and half the johns don't work. The showers are nasty, and water runs on the floor 'cause them drains is clogged. I don't bother with that cafeteria. I hear they put roaches in the food. But that ain't nothin'. I seen roaches before. But Coach says we got to get us C's to play ball. So, Miz Weaver, what we got to do to get us our C in here?"

He glanced back at the three young men in the back of the room, and they made it a refrain. "What we got to do to get us our C?"

Penny regretted asking them how they liked St. Francis, but too late now. "Open your books, and I'll show you exactly what I expect. The midterm exam is only a few weeks away, so we have a lot of work to do."

Then the chorus: "I don't have no book."

"Someone stole my book."

"I don't have no money."

"They ain't give us our money yet."

Penny held up her hand and waited until they settled. "How many have the text book?" She pointed to the board where she'd written its title. Out of seventeen students, five raised their hands. "You need books. There will be homework." She pointed to the assignment. "And open book tests. When you come to class Thursday, I expect you to have your book, paper, something to write with, and your homework."

"Miss, do you grade our homework?" asked Lashandra.

"I do. Now those with books, let's look at the chapters we will cover. I'll bring a syllabus Thursday, too. She looked at her seating chart. "Sheila, which chapters had your other teacher, Ms. Avery, already covered?"

Sheila looked over at her neighbor's book, then up at Penny. "She ain't use no book. She just give us assignments, tole us to check liberry books out and write our papers on them. We ain't needed no book."

"You need a book now," said Penny. "So we start with chapter one."

The whole class groaned.

At 9:00 a.m. she was going over the homework assignment for Thursday when Lashandra got up, snatched up her book bag, and walked out. Before she could react, Sheila had followed her out. When Terence started to rise along with some of the muscular boys in the back row, she said fiercely, "If anyone else leaves, you'll be counted absent. You need to be here at eight when class begins. If you're not here by ten after eight, you'll also be counted absent without excuse."

The boys sat back down. Ronny and Merilee were whispering, but everyone else was sulkily quiet. Only twelve more minutes to go.

~

"I knew I had to be tough," Penny said to Oscar, who had urged her to come to his office and tell him how it went, "but maybe I overreacted. Should I have let them go to the bathroom?"

Oscar laughed, leaned back in his chair, and put his feet on his desk. "It's a problem," he said. "These students don't seem to have much control over their bladders. Sounds like Lashandra and Sheila were testing you, though. I've told mine to stop at the bathroom on their way to class. If they have to leave during class, then don't come back. Did Terence give you any problems? He was late. By the way, I found several students in the hall when I left a little before 8:30. I told them to be on time, or they could expect an F. Jane Avery was very slipshod about attendance and lateness. In fact, one student told me she was often late herself."

"She must have let them go early a lot, too," said Penny. "They weren't expecting to be there the whole seventy-five minutes." It helped so much to talk these things over with Oscar.

"That's why you've got nine weeks to get through fourteen weeks' worth of material. But I'm sure you can do it. Watch Terence. I had to throw him out of my class. He fell asleep the second week, sitting right there in the first row, just like he was today. He was even snoring, which is why I noticed. I get so involved in my lecture, I sometimes don't keep my eye on all the students. I jerked him to his feet and told him if he slept in my class again, I'd toss him out." Oscar was grinning.

"Really?" Penny was trying to picture it. Oscar was wiry and fit but half a foot shorter than Terence, who was well over six feet.

"I did, and the next time the class met, he did it again. And I did throw him right out, pushed him out into the hall and told him never to return to my class."

Penny laughed. What a relief that Oscar had discipline problems, too. "I don't think I could use that strategy."

"Probably not, but you'll have to be tough and consistent. A lot of these kids come from the inner cities, places like Camden, New Jersey, and D.C., both tough towns. They don't even hear you when you're nice and polite, unless you've made it clear that you're the one in authority. You'll do fine. They'll end up loving you." He gave her a very endearing smile, which should have warned her.

"I hope so," she said, "and be able to teach them something. If they couldn't pass the entrance exams, why are they here?"

Oscar got up, walked around, and shut his door. He needed privacy to answer her questions?

"They take everybody here," he said, "give them tests and put most of these entering freshman into remedial courses, high school English and Math. They call them Developmental courses now. They weren't even doing that until a year ago, but they had to do it to keep their accreditation. Some of your Pre-Comp students can't read even at middle school level. The Reading teachers are frustrated out of their minds. But these kids have a chance now to catch up, if they'll buckle down and work. I think you'll get some to do that." He walked back and forth in the narrow area between his desk and the bookcases on the wall to the right of the door.

"It turned out Terence should never have been in my Freshman Comp class to start with. He made very low scores on both the reading and writing placement tests. His advisor put him in my class, probably under pressure from the football coach. He has a sports scholarship, if he can keep his grades to a C average, but I doubt that he can, even if he works hard. He's too far behind. He bragged to me that he made his living selling drugs in Camden before he came here. You'll need to be alert with him. He's a very skilled con artist."

Penny stared at the plant with its heart-shaped leaves spilling down the side of Oscar's bookcase. What had she gotten herself into? She'd been in a lot of difficult situations, but drug pushers? This might be beyond even her ingenuity. Certainly, it was beyond her experience.

"I don't know why I trust you so much or am so sure you can handle these kids," he went on. "You know I'm the only African American in the English Department. Their last chairman, who was white, quit, couldn't take the way the administration treated him. Some of the teachers are fine. They know their subjects, but they're not connecting well with these kids. I went around the first day of class to watch through the windows in the classroom doors. Most of our instructors don't even make eye contact with the students. I watched you, too, after I left."

He was smiling. She was glad she hadn't known he'd been watching her.

"You looked at them, Penny. You engaged them. Yes, they gave you a hard time, but they cared enough to do that. They're not bad kids, even Terence, but they need order in their lives—discipline and especially people who care enough about them to help them believe they'll succeed."

Penny couldn't believe he had read her so well in such a short time. She felt a little dizzy with his faith in her, as if she were floating or suspended. She didn't usually get this much praise from someone she had known barely two days. "I tell my students, if you don't want me to believe in you, go away," she said quietly.

"Exactly." He went back to pacing, then stared out the window a few minutes and turned back to her. "For these kids, this is not only their chance to turn their lives around. It's their last chance. Most mornings I pass a busload of prisoners near that prison at the city limits. It always makes me so sad. I see the despair in their faces. That's where Ronny and Terence and these others are going to end up if they don't make it here."

Penny held his eyes until he looked away. She couldn't help herself. He was so intense, and she felt caught up in the sadness he was letting show in his eyes. It made her want to comfort him, but how? This sudden intimacy surprised her, but it worried her, too. He talked to her like she was his wife, for cat's sake.

He walked over and sat down again at his desk. She glanced at her watch. "I have my seminar in ten minutes. Were you going to introduce me there, too?"

"Of course. It's around the corner in 407. That's a good group. I met with them last week. You won't have any trouble there. What I'm really worried about, Penny, is the President. I can't get the English Department budget numbers."

Again Penny was startled. She was brand new, and he was already confiding in her his problem with the President? She must have looked her surprise because he smiled. "I told you I trusted you, and you're the only one around here. I've talked to Rick about this. He trusts you, too. Actually, I can't believe I do. I can count on the fingers of one hand the white people I've been close to in my life."

He was getting to her too fast and far too effectively. She and Rick had a long history of working together for ten years on community issues: nuclear safety, air pollution, and a stressful political campaign. Their closeness had developed over time, and his wife, Cathy, had been her best friend even longer, but she had met Oscar yesterday. True, it wasn't the first time she had been trusted in an unexpected way. She must convey something to people that she wasn't aware of. But this developing closeness made her uncomfortable even though she was flattered.

"Do you mind?" he asked.

"No." She smiled in spite of herself and saw his shoulders relax. At that moment someone tapped on the door and pushed it open. A plump woman with neatly permed grey-blonde hair and rimless square glasses stuck her head in, glanced at Penny, and said, "Oscar, I need to see you."

Penny saw anger flash across his face. Then he walked to the door, pulled it all the way open and faced her, so that she backed up a little. "Blanche, this is not a good time. Let me introduce you to Penny Weaver, our new adjunct. She's replacing Jane Avery. She just started today, so we're going over some things." He sounded stiff and formal, so different from how he was when he talked to her.

Blanche nodded. She took her glasses off as if to get a better look at Penny and let them fall onto her bosom, where they were held by a gold chain around her neck.

"I'm Professor Rowan. Oscar, I must see you as soon as possible. It's about the summer school schedule."

"I'll be busy until well after ten, Blanche." Oscar had his hand on the door knob as though eager to close it. "I can see you here at 10:30. I'm introducing Penny to her Creative Writing seminar at 10:00. I don't see the rush, Blanche. I haven't even begun working on the summer school schedule."

"It's due in two weeks," Blanche said, "before spring break. Hadn't you better begin discussions with the faculty? I've always taught World Lit in the summer."

"We can discuss that at 10:30," Oscar said firmly. "Excuse me now, Blanche. I do need to go over some things with Penny."

"Why did you give her the Creative Writing seminar? I thought–"

"She's a published poet, Blanche. Now please excuse us, and come back at 10:30."

Blanche gave Penny a hard look, as though to discover her qualifications for teaching anything. She did not look one bit impressed. Penny knew she was not much to look at, but she never made much effort with her clothes, wore no makeup. She liked to be herself and low key.

Then Blanche returned her glasses to her nose and turned away, her heels clicking on the outer office linoleum as she walked away, without saying anything else.

Oscar shut the door quietly and locked it. His shoulders sagged. Penny waited. She had seen by her watch that they had four minutes to get to room 407. She hoped she was ready for those students.

He stood close to her and spoke quietly. "That was Blanche Rowan, another of my problems. But anyway, back to President Siler, who won't give me my departmental budget. I've been up the ladder. The Arts and Humanities Division Head can't get hers either, but she's not even trying. She smiles and does whatever she's told. I've pressed the Finance Officer, Rob Grubb. He won't return my calls, or he barricades himself in his office. According to his secretary, it's not a convenient time, but apparently it never is. I've been in to see him a dozen times, and it's always inconvenient. The Provost admits I need a budget to run my department, but she says, 'Give it time. I'll talk to her.' What does all that sound like, Penny?"

"Sounds fishy," said Penny and stood up. After all her insistence to the students not to be late, she didn't want to be late herself.

"Absolutely right." Oscar beamed, then whispered, "Someone's mismanaging the college budget, and it must be pretty high up, if not the President herself."

Two

Tuesday, February 13. Penny had agreed to meet her friend Sammie in the foyer of Booher Hall at 3:00. Sammie Hargrave taught History and Sociology and shared her office with other full-time instructors on the third floor. Penny had just picked up a copy of the student newspaper, *The Winged Messenger*, from the stand by the door when Sammie came up behind her and put her arm around her. "So good to have you here, girl. Come on, let's go home. I'm ready to drop."

Sammie wore a red pantsuit with heels and earrings to match, a white silk blouse with lace cuffs, and a page boy wig. Penny always had to take a minute to adjust to Sammie's new look. She never looked the same. The clothes, the hair, the shoes, the earrings—it all changed daily. For Penny clothes were simply things you put on that were as reasonably priced, comfortable, clean and appropriate as she could manage, but for Sammie, her appearance represented a new presentation of herself every day.

Sammie pushed open one of the heavy front doors and led the way down to the sidewalk to College Avenue. It was surprisingly warm for mid-February, in the high sixties, if not seventy. Daffodils were opening in the flower gardens in front of the building.

"How did it go?" asked Sammie as they wove around a few small groups of students chatting near the steps and on the sidewalk.

"Not too bad. As soon as Oscar left, they started testing me in the eight o'clock. The ten o'clock, Creative Writing, was easy. I've got Obie Warren in there, and he sets a respectful tone. You knew he was Assistant Football Coach here now?"

"Oh, yes, and we're lucky to get him. Truth be known, he's better than Coach Cox. He can get more out of the kids. He started last August when I did. That is good, that he'll take Creative Writing. He has a good mind, but you know that. What about your freshmen? What did they get up to?"

Penny related the girls' need to leave early and to go to the bathroom, and Sammie was laughing so hard, she staggered in her heels. Penny put out a hand to keep her from falling.

"You *are* tough, girl. Not let them go to the bathroom?" She went off into more peals of laughter. She was wiping her eyes when they got to College Avenue, where she was parked.

"I probably overdid it," said Penny as she waited for Sammie to unlock her door. It felt so good to laugh with Sammie. All the stresses of the morning rolled right off her.

Sammie shook her head and walked around to the driver's side to slide in under the steering wheel. She looked at Penny and grinned. "No, tough is good here. Start tough, and loosen up later once they settle down. Nice doesn't cut it, especially not when you start five weeks late. That's hard, girl, but you'll be just what they need. Don't kid yourself. They know you care about them. At least you have a good chairman. Mine is the pits. Ed Clarkson. He could care less what happens to the students or the faculty he's supposed to take care of."

"But you cope," said Penny as Sammie pulled out into traffic.

"Oh, yes, I like teaching. I like the kids. I wish Clarkson would let me start some Women's Studies courses, do more with Black History. He's old and useless. He teaches the one and only Black History course–by rote, I think. It puts the kids to sleep, if you can believe it. Then he has the Beginning American History. He's got me doing two sections of Sociology I, European History, and World History, plus Freshman Studies. World History is okay, but European is dull. All those greedy colonialists."

"I'm glad I have only two courses," Penny said. "Oscar thinks I can catch them up to where they should be, so I'm going to be stepping."

Sammie signaled a turn and took the on ramp for I-40, heading west for Shagbark County. "You'll do it, and Oscar will be at your back the whole way. That's the way he is. I envy you guys in English your supportive chairman. Mine not only doesn't give a rat's ass about us or the kids, but he tries to get in all the girls' pants."

Sammie was in the far left lane and speeding past all the traffic. It wouldn't take long to get home at this rate. "He gets away with it?" Penny was familiar with academics who were cutthroat with each other as they worked their way up the promotion ladder, but she hadn't run into the problem of professors seducing students at the community college.

"Not if I can help it," said Sammie.

Penny thought of Oscar. Could he intend to seduce her? No, it didn't feel like that, but it would be hard to explain to Kenneth, especially the part about how he was affecting her. She glanced at the speedometer. They were going eighty miles an hour, fifteen over the speed limit. Sammie had kicked off her shoes. They were already on Highway 64. Thirty more minutes to Riverdell, or less. "What will you do?"

"I haven't figured that out exactly, but I've told my classes that they can talk to me about anything, and I'm hoping more of them will bring this up. Merilee has already come in and spilled the beans."

"Merilee Taylor?"

"Yes. Why? Do you have her, too?"

"It must be the same girl. I have her in pre-comp at eight. She was fine. It was two other girls, Lashandra and Sheila, who declared class over at nine and walked out."

"Because they couldn't use the john? Oh, Penny, what we gonna do wid you?"

"Let me be your co-conspirator, I guess, and teach me your tricks. Merilee was sitting by Ronny Glover, a football player with balloons for arms."

"I haven't had him," said Sammie, "but if his muscles look pumped, he's probably on steroids."

"So that's it," said Penny. "He can barely walk. Says he's here to play football. His first semester, and he hopes not to be kicked out."

"He's not off to a good start," Sammie said grimly. "Merilee shouldn't be hanging around with anyone like that. She came in because she has flunked the first two tests in Sociology I, and she's worried about passing. She asked me about extra credit. I said I couldn't give more than five percent. Penny, she made seven percent on one test and fifteen percent on another one. So I went over the test with her, and guess what? She can't read, at least not above third grade level. I recommended she get a tutor and sent her to the Lower College, where they have some, though I don't know how good they are. She shouldn't even be in college."

"How will she pass a composition course if she can't read? I don't get it." Penny wondered how many others among her students were similarly handicapped. Of course, they would look for ways to distract her.

"I do," said Sammie. They had slowed to go through Pittsboro and around the courthouse circle. "After she left I looked up her transcript. All passing grades in high school, but she was in Special Ed. She started here last fall. She made an A in Music. That's basically chorus, an easy A. If they show up and sing, they get an A. But she made an A in American History with Clarkson. How do you figure?"

"She's cheating?"

"Maybe. She gave me some homework with perfect answers. She said her roommate helped her. I told her homework was practicing for tests. She needed to do it herself. It didn't count that much, but if she copied, even on homework, she'd get an F and could get kicked out of the class. The college does have rules for cheating." She smiled at Penny.

"You're mean, too."

"You betcha. It's a cold, cruel world out there for these kids if they can't read or write."

"But you said she shouldn't be in college. It's too late for her to learn to read here, isn't it?"

"Oh, Penny. I love you for so many reasons, but you always say it so straight. Of course, you're right. But how did she get an A in History from that bastard who's my chair?"

"I have no idea."

"If it's not cheating, what else could it be but sex? Anyway, she practically admitted it. Said he helped her outside of class and told her if she'd do some things for him, he'd guarantee an A. She gave me a sweet little smile. She wanted some deal with me. I told her, 'No deals. You work for grades in my class. You master the material. It's called studying, and then you pass the course.'"

"What did she say?"

Sammie didn't answer until she'd turned right at the light and onto 87 North. It always cheered Penny to see the sign on the outskirts of Pittsboro: Riverdell 15 miles. Kenneth would be waiting to hear about how it had gone. What in the world would she say about Oscar? If she said anything, he'd read her in a minute. He knew her too well. She tuned back into Sammie who was saying, "She started crying. I hate it when they cry. Where does the college get these kids anyway? When I was coming up, they'd never have come close to being admitted to a college. These HBCUs used to be respectable. Malvina tells how in the 1960s St. Francis took only the top students from the black high schools. Now we've got the dregs, and they're pitiful besides."

"Not all, surely?"

"No, not all, but about half the student body isn't going to make it. They're too far behind, or they've never opened a book in their lives. They're bright and think they can wing it on their intelligence. There's even a rumor going around that the surest way to flunk out is to do your homework, that if you want an A, don't bother going to class."

"That's a new one," said Penny. "I do have several students who came to class without pencil, paper or textbook."

Sammie had made a left onto the Riverdell Road. "Tell me about it. I give open book tests, and if no paper or book, they have to leave and take their F."

"I guess tough is best. By the way, that one young man with no book or writing materials, Terence, had a mouthful of gold teeth. I've never seen that in someone so young."

"Cocaine habit," said Sammie. "Rotted all his teeth."

At shortly after 3:30 Sammie drove them up the Ho Chi Minh Trail, as their former neighbor May Madison had called it because of all the potholes. No more potholes at 7 Whitfield Mill Road, but the name had stuck. Penny and Kenneth rented the garage apartment from Belle Jones during their months in the states, normally March through August. Kenneth was outside talking to Malvina and Cathy, who were standing near Cathy's van with the basketball and soccer stickers on the back. Her sons, Neill and Joe, were playing at the hoop at the edge of the parking lot. School got out at 3:00. They must have just arrived. They all walked over to greet Penny, who was seeing them for the first time since she and Kenneth had gotten back from Wales.

"The profs arrive!" sang out Cathy. Her real pageboy, not a wig, was held back by a wide gold ribbon that brought out the gold flecks in her eyes and in her brown, hand-knitted sweater. She hurried over to hug Penny as she climbed out of the car. "Too long! I missed you so much," she whispered.

Penny laughed. "It's good to be back. I missed you, too." She turned to Malvina to hug her. Malvina wore a loose-fitting cotton dress with bright African colors over her ample figure. As she squeezed her friend, she said, "Welcome back, Penny. We want to hear all about your first day."

"Come on up then, everybody," said Kenneth, giving Penny his own hug and a quick kiss. She was so relieved to be back inside their familiar and well-tested love. That was what she needed and all she needed. Period.

Penny turned to Neill and Joe, who were waiting to say hello. Neill, at almost fourteen, was skinnier than ever and shooting up, and Joe at ten, once plump, was not far behind Neill in height and more slender. "You guys want to come up and have a snack or keep on playing pick up?"

They both hugged Penny, and while Joe dribbled the ball, Neill explained that they'd wait for the twins next door to get home from school. They'd promised to watch them while their mom Jan did some errands.

"Good," said Penny, "but come on up if you get hungry."

"Mrs. Style will probably feed us," chimed in Joe. "She always does, but thanks. We'll wait for Penny and Kenny's school bus."

Penny followed her guests upstairs. In some ways she would rather have collapsed in a chair with only Kenneth to listen. She had learned as much from Sammie on the drive home as she had from her two classes and Oscar's worries, but Cathy and Malvina were dear friends and very invested in her new teaching job. They would have perspective for her because they knew the college, and she did need to learn all she could, the faster, the better, to keep ahead of her students. She hoped she could do it as well as Oscar and Sammie believed she could.

By the time she walked through the screen door, Kenneth was handing around juice and ice water. "I can make tea," he said, but the others shook their heads. "What for you, love?"

"Juice sounds great. Wow, guys, what a day. After meeting my students, I thought I saw my main challenges, but Sammie has been filling me in on stuff I never imagined."

"Tell, tell," said Cathy, leaning forward, her eyes bright with interest.

The phone rang twenty minutes after they had settled in to hear Penny's first day experiences and Sammie's take on her chairman versus Penny's, her worries about ignorant freshmen girls like Merilee. Kenneth handed the phone to Penny. Their apartment was small, and their three guests filled it up. They had a long cord so they could move the phone around as needed. Penny got up and walked over to stand near the outside door. "Obie, hi. What can I do for you?"

Sammie called out, "Tell him to come over and join our brainstorming. Tell him you've got some of his football boys."

Penny held up a hand. "It's not hard, Obie, to start your autobiography. For Thursday I only want five to ten pages. You can begin with your birth or with your parents or grandparents. You can even begin where you are now and then go back to the beginning of your life. I'm sure it will be fine. Listen, I've been talking with Sammie Hargrave,

Cathy Clegg and Malvina Johnson about some of the problems at the college. We'd love for you to join us. Now, actually, if you're free. That would be great. Bring Delois, too, if she's home. Oh, okay. See you soon then." She hung up the phone. "He'll come right over. He has to pick up Delois at 5:30. She's staying late at the school for a staff meeting."

"Great," said Sammie. "I'm curious how he's doing with Coach Cox. Obie's a hundred times smarter."

"Oscar said Cox pushed an advisor into putting Terence, one of my students, into regular Freshman Comp, when he should have had the Pre-Comp course. So I have Terence now. Oscar says he made his college money selling drugs in Camden."

Penny could tell by the frown on Kenneth's face that this worried him. It probably hadn't occurred to him that some of her students would be drug dealers. It hadn't occurred to her either.

"He probably sells on campus, too," said Sammie. "Can I get anyone else a juice refill?"

Kenneth jumped up, but Sammie beat him to the refrigerator, so he shifted his kitchen chair so he could add another one for Obie. He caught Penny's eye and shook his head.

"It's a problem at all the colleges," said Malvina, "white, black, Ivy League, church colleges. Date rape, too. Camden is a very tough town. It's a miracle these kids from Camden get into college at all, from what I've heard."

"Merilee's from Camden, too," said Penny, looking at Sammie.

"I didn't know. What about the steroids guy?"

"Ronny? He's from Camden, too."

"Steroids?" asked Cathy. "You mean taking them to pump up his muscles for sports? Isn't that illegal?"

"Yes," said Sammie, "very illegal. Let's ask Obie about that, too. Oh, I hear a car. I bet that's him."

Kenneth went to the door, and in minutes Obie had joined them, tall, slender, smiling, his grey eyes happy. "I'm honored," he said. "All these beautiful women with good minds and hearts." He accepted ice water and sat down next to Kenneth. "Have you talked about the football team yet?"

"We'd only got started," said Cathy, who had known Obie and his wife Delois the longest, as they had grown up in Riverdell and were part of the Ebenezer Baptist family where Rick was pastor. "Tell us your take. You've had your first season there as Assistant Coach. I know St. Francis lost a lot of games. How do you see the problems?"

"Too many to solve all at once," he said, setting his water on the coffee table. "Top on my list is getting them serious about their studies so I have a team and don't lose my good ones because their grades bottom out. I'm personally doing their study hall with them two nights a week to be sure they're getting their assignments done. I was surprised some of the freshmen didn't have any grades yet when I sent around progress reports for their English class. Ms. Avery? Any of you know her?"

Sammie laughed. "She was fired, and Penny has taken over her English 21 students, and she's got some of yours, all right—Terence, Ronny. Don't Ronny's pumped muscles worry you?"

"Oh, so Ms. Avery is gone?"

Penny nodded. "I started today. I have the eight o'clock, and Ronny, Terence and at least three other freshman football players, maybe more, are in it."

Obie frowned. "You'll push them, right? I mean, you'll work them like you're making us write in Creative Writing?"

"Yes, my students will have to work to pass, and that 21 class is five weeks behind. I'm glad you'll be making sure they do their homework. That could make all the difference. I don't get the impression that my freshman students are used to studying."

Kenneth looked puzzled, Obie grinned, and Sammie laughed.

"Now wait here just a doggone minute," said Malvina. "My niece Letitia is a second semester freshman at St. Francis, and honor roll. She graduated from Riverdell High, Valedictorian. Don't be running down this college now. It has some good teachers. Lookee here, Penny, you and Sammie are the best. Those kids don't know yet how lucky they are. Then Oscar Farrell. He graduated from UC Berkeley in English. And Obie's their coach and is going to make sure they get their work done. I don't mean no harm, but this new crop of freshmen is lucky. Problems, yes, the black community always has problems, but these young people have such an opportunity, and don't any of y'all forget it."

Obie smiled at Penny, but Sammie looked abashed. Had Penny ever seen her look like she wanted to crawl into a hole and disappear? She couldn't remember that she had. Not bouncy, land-on-her-feet Sammie. Penny had seen Malvina scold other people, especially white people, but she had never before been the recipient of her righteous anger, and apparently, Sammie hadn't either. She hoped Sammie wouldn't ever be again. Penny wasn't sure how to respond. The problems were real, for sure. She looked at Kenneth, who caught her eye and smiled. He liked this tack better. He didn't like hearing about drug sales or seductive professors.

"Anyone want more juice?" he asked.

They shifted in their seats, shook their heads. Sammie stood. "I need to get back. Penny, want to ride in with me Thursday? Save Kenneth a trip?"

"Sure. I need to be there by eight or before."

"Let's leave from here at 6:30. I like to go early and beat the Raleigh traffic."

"Good. Thanks."

Obie stood, too. "I'd better be off to pick up Delois. Thanks for having me."

Cathy said, "But we didn't get to hear about your work and how you're doing with the coaching."

Obie shook his head, looked at Malvina. "I know, Miss Malvina, that we have some very good students like Letitia. You must be proud of her. It's true that we have some outstanding professors, two in this room. I had my first writing class with Miss Penny today, and I can't wait to get home and start my autobiography."

Malvina beamed, and Penny thought how dear this young man was to be so good with all of them, who were at least a generation older.

"But you know, Miss Malvina," Obie continued, "the college is letting in some young folks who don't know how to act, who didn't get good raisin' like you and me and all us here did. They been treated bad, and they treat other people bad, teachers and coaches, too. I love my football

boys, but I have to watch them every minute, and I can't
live at the college. I have to come home sometimes. They
sell drugs behind my back. I know Terence does and
Ronny, too. I know Ronny's on steroids. Coach won't do
anything because he's a freshman and has to get his grades
up before he can play. Coach don't want to waste his time.
They rape girls, too. You can call it date rape, but it's still
rape, ain't it?

"And they fight. They 'bout kill each other sometimes.
Just this afternoon I had to break up a fight in the football
dorm between Terence and another guy, and Terence had
his knife out. I barely got there in time. It's scary, you
know? It scares me, and I don't scare easy. I 'preciate Miss
Penny and Miss Sammie for teaching these kids, but it ain't
easy, Miss Malvina, it sure ain't easy."

The whole time he talked, Malvina had been smiling
her encouragement as if she could lift him up with her
smile. "I know it's hard, Obie. You keep on working with
these young people, and Penny and Sammie, too. I know
y'all will make a big difference. But remember the positive
side. Look past all the junk. They don't know any better.
They need exactly what you're giving them, good adult
models. Your influence will last them all their lives."

Penny stood as Obie and Sammie moved toward the
door. After she and Kenneth had waved them off, she sat
down and took up the conversation again. "Malvina, I hear
you, and I want to learn all I can. If I can get through to
them, I think I can teach these kids some writing skills. But
I'm not getting through yet."

"You will," said Cathy. She glanced at Malvina. She
and Penny both looked to Malvina as an elder statesman.
She had been Rick Clegg's campaign manager in 1998,

when he ran for Shagbark County Commissioner and won. Malvina had never lost faith in Rick or in what they were doing to shift county government to a more responsible, forward-thinking basis, dark as those days had been. If Malvina and Cathy believed she'd succeed, she'd try to quiet her doubts, and Kenneth's. He still looked worried.

"Penny," said Malvina, "they need your skills. They're still children. They'll soak up things about you that you don't even know you have. And you have Oscar to support you. That's a very bright star there in the St. Francis crown. Obie and Sammie don't have that kind of support behind them." She set her glass on the coffee table. "I know you'll struggle some, but what a great gift you'll give these young people. Keep your eye on that."

Penny looked at Kenneth. He looked like he wanted to argue. She turned back to Malvina. "Oscar is helpful, but he's frustrated about President Siler. He wants to make things better, but he says she blocks him."

Malvina leaned back. "I've been following Siler. She's new, too, two years ago. Angus Brown, the old man they had for forty years, was the real incompetent. I don't say she's perfect, but she's better. He's the one let everything go downhill. He ran the college bankrupt. They nearly lost their accreditation two years ago. Give her a chance. She's building up the football team, which will help pull in more alumni money. Tell Oscar to give her some maneuvering room. Lot of HBCUs going under now. She's trying to save a good school."

Then Malvina did launch herself to a standing position and walked over to hug Penny and Kenneth, as did Cathy, following in her wake. "Call me," whispered Cathy. "Penny, I know it will work out. You can tame anybody."

Penny laughed and squeezed her. She remembered that quote she loved from *The Little Prince*. "You are responsible for what you have tamed." Could she tame the balloon muscles and the mouthful of gold teeth? If she could, what in the world would she do with them?

Three

Thursday, February 15. The following Thursday Sammie got Penny to the college shortly after seven. Fortunately, the building was unlocked at seven, so she could go up to her classroom. Sammie hugged her, wished her luck with her "babies," and went off to her office to prepare for her nine o'clock.

Penny flicked on the classroom lights of 402, erased the inscrutable, perhaps obscene, student drawings on the chalk board, and settled at the desk. She had already prepared for class, so she took out her thermos of coffee and her diary. Maybe she could sort out how she was going to manage working with Oscar and holding him at a more comfortable distance.

The night before Kenneth had rampaged about the drugs and the student who resorted to knives, but that was nothing to how he would react if he knew how Oscar had made her his confidante instantly. She didn't mind listening to Oscar, but he was stirring her deeply by trusting her with all this knowledge she wouldn't ordinarily have access to, knowledge that could ruin lives or reputations. Knowledge is power, she had realized years ago. He was giving her power she didn't want as a lowly adjunct. Why couldn't he see that? But it was hard not to listen, not to care about him because of his total trust in her. She wished she could name better what was happening between them. If she didn't understand it, how could Kenneth possibly? She purposely had not gone down to the English Department office to check her mail in case he was there early, too. She would go after class. She needed time to think before she saw him again.

But Oscar walked in five minutes later. "You're early. Like me." He walked over to the front of her desk. "I like to get here before anybody else." He smiled as though nothing delighted him more than finding her alone at 7:15 in the morning.

Goddesses, help me, she thought. I'm in over my head here. "I ride in with Sammie Hargrave in History." She would try to put things on a very ordinary, even boring, footing between them. "She's a good friend in Riverdell, she and her husband Derek, who works with our Shagbark County Sheriff's Department."

"She's new here? Lively? Attractive? Wants to do Women's Studies? I did meet her last fall. Our paths don't cross much, but I've been thinking maybe English and History could do a joint Women's Studies seminar, literature by women and the history of feminism."

"Oh, she'd love that. Talk to her about it. She did her thesis through the Women's Studies program at UNC on the part African Americans have played in the feminist struggle. Sammie and I have worked together on environmental issues and a tough political campaign–you know, Rick's–when he ran for Commissioner. She and Derek are Deacons in Rick's church."

Oscar was pacing. He walked to a blackboard near the door and picked up an eraser. He apparently didn't want to pursue the subject of Women's Studies or church deacons right now. He ran the eraser over the board Penny had already erased. Then he turned. "Mind if I close the door? I want to ask your opinion."

"Okay," she said. She did mind. She was happy to listen to him. It was flattering, but she didn't want him pulling her any closer. Small hope that wouldn't happen. But what was she going to do, walk out? Say, "Yes, I mind"? No. Why did he need to close the door? Wasn't the building empty, for goodness sake?

"I think I might have really lost it yesterday with Audrey." He stood straight as a soldier at attention in front of her.

"Audrey?"

"Audrey White, the Provost. I lost my temper, to put it mildly."

Oh, that Audrey. What was she supposed to know about that? He sat down in a student desk opposite her. She waited. Even if she didn't want to know, he was going to tell her. She had visions of him throwing the Provost out of his office or hers. He had thrown Terence out for sleeping. Did he throw Provosts, too?

"You have Merilee Taylor, right? The young woman who was sitting next to Ronny in the back row last Tuesday when I introduced you?"

"Yes. Sammie has her, too. She was telling me–"

"I found out yesterday that Edmund Clarkson, the History Department Chair," he said, using the title with contempt, "has been sleeping with Merilee. He promised her an A if she would."

"I heard."

"You knew?" He looked astonished.

"Sammie told me Tuesday afternoon. She has Merilee in Sociology. Sammie's feeling pretty bad about her. She says Merilee can barely read at third grade level."

Oscar shook his head. "So a department head comes along and victimizes her? It makes me want to get the hell out of here so fast your head would spin."

Penny leaned back in her chair. "But you're still here."

"I'm here, and I'll see that bastard fired."

Penny guessed where this was leading. He had gone to the Provost to get Clarkson fired. She'd read over the faculty rules for sexual conduct only the night before. Students were off limits.

"Can you do that? Sammie would be happy. She says there's more than this one incident, and he's a poor chairman to boot." That was putting it mildly.

"He can't be fired without the President's permission, but Mrs. Christine Siler is working at home and won't be back in her office until Monday. So I went to Audrey. Sometimes I can get Audrey to see my point of view, and she has Siler's ear. I stayed calm. I told her what I'd learned from Merilee's roommate. That's Letitia Harrelson. She's a freshman English major. You have her in your writing seminar."

"Oh, yes, I think I know which one she is, and she's from Riverdell, too, and niece of another good friend of mine."

Oscar got up and began pacing again. "Letitia is very smart, an excellent student, has had both her comp classes with me, and got my permission to do your seminar. I trust her completely."

"Did you also talk to Merilee?"

"I did, before I tried to talk to the President." He walked over to the window and looked out. Penny looked at her watch. Quarter of eight. She'd have students soon.

"Merilee confirmed it?"

"Oh, yes. Such an innocent, so afraid she'll fail, she'll do anything for a grade. I don't think she realizes how Clarkson is abusing her. It makes me so angry. She might as well be a child. There's some kind of mental problem."

"She's learning disabled, Sammie says."

"Probably retarded, too." He flung himself back into the chair opposite her desk.

Someone knocked at the door. Penny glanced at the window in it. It looked like Lashandra. "Students," she said. "I'd better get the assignment up on the board."

"They can wait a minute. The President was nowhere to be found. She wasn't answering her phone at home either. I told Audrey that was unacceptable. The college had a serious infraction of faculty conduct rules, and the President needed to deal with it, and you know what Audrey said? 'If we fired all the staff who've broken the sexual conduct rules, we'd lose half the faculty.' Then I just lost it."

~

One happy student, no, two, made up for her eighteen disgruntled ones in the eight o'clock that morning. Lashandra and Sheila, although they'd acted resentful during class, stayed after class to apologize for walking out the Tuesday before, and Lashandra said, "I like the Creative Writing class better. In my Journalism courses, we do a lot of writing, Ms. Weaver, and I love to write, but I hate writing compositions. Plus, reading is a pain. I was so angry I had to do Pre-Comp again. It wasn't your fault."

"Again?" Penny asked.

Lashandra looked at Sheila and then back at Penny. "I flunked it last fall. I hated those papers we had to write. I don't like to count paragraphs and make topic sentences. I want to write my feelings as they come to me."

"That's probably why you failed," said Penny, "and composition is an important skill. Now reading is the single most important thing you can do to be a good writer. I'll see you shortly in Creative Writing. The two courses should go well together. What you learn in Pre-Comp will help you write better in your Creative Writing and Journalism assignments, too."

Penny was packed up, but the girls were in no hurry to end the conversation. Sheila glanced at Lashandra and said, "I wish I could take Creative Writing. My advisor said I had to wait till next year and get all these prerequisites out of the way." She stuck out her tongue.

Penny laughed. "Probably wise. You'll both do fine in here. You're intelligent. All you have to do is study, but that's why you're in college, right?"

"Me," said Sheila, "I came for the boys."

Lashandra poked her in the ribs. "Be serious."

"I want my degree," said Sheila, "but I plan on enjoying these boys and finding me a good steady boyfriend, a good bed warmer."

"Shut your mouth, girl. What Miz Weaver gonna think?"

"She gonna think I'm average," said Sheila. "C'mon, let's go study." She looked at Penny and stuck out her tongue again. Penny laughed as Lashandra pushed her out the door.

Penny had lifted her backpack from the desk and picked up her coat and scarf when a tall, slightly stooped white man strode into the room, pushing a large cart with a TV on it. He said, "You're leaving?"

"Yes."

"I need to get in here and set up before my 9:30."

"No problem. I was leaving."

Then he stopped and stared at her intensely. He had such thick glasses that she wondered if he was having trouble seeing her. "I haven't seen you before. You teach the Tuesday-Thursday eight o'clock in here? I thought Jane Avery was the teacher."

"No, she's gone. It's her class I took over last Tuesday. I'm Penny Weaver."

He ran his hand over his very black hair (dyed?) and stared as if he couldn't fit the information into the right slot. "Penny Weaver? You're an adjunct? English?"

"Yes. Professor Farrell hired me Monday."

"I see. How are you finding it, teaching here?"

"So far, so good. They're not testing me now. They've turned sullen." She laughed.

"Sounds familiar," he said. "I've taught here thirty years. I'm Ed Clarkson, by the way, Chair of the History Department."

Penny smiled inwardly. Sammie's hated Chair, Merilee's seducer, and the man who set Oscar's teeth on edge. Clarkson looked pretty impotent to stir so much strong feeling. He was one of the least appetizing men she'd ever seen. Mostly flab, and he didn't seem quite present.

"You'll get used to it," he said. "I started out idealistic, but I soon learned. They don't start studying until after the midterm, so I don't bother much until then. Movies, maps, a few things, but nothing serious. When they start coming to class, worried they'll flunk, then I start serious teaching."

Penny could not think of a single thing to say. He had been at this college thirty years? Why had they kept him? Why had he stayed?

He was watching her, running his hands over his hair, then over his eyebrows. His staring was disconcerting.

"I'd better get out of your way." She picked up her backpack.

"Oh, don't rush off. They're never on time. I usually start about quarter of ten. I have to get this movie organized is all." He took off his limp sports jacket with leather elbow patches and hung it over the chair beside the teacher's desk. Then he pulled the cart over. "Farrell seems okay. The guy before him was going crazy with frustration. Little piece of advice." He stepped closer to her. "Don't try to change anything. Nothing changes here. 2001 is very similar to 1971. Kids are here against their will. Parents make them come. The kids don't give a damn about their education. Half of them are high all the time. The other half are stupid. They take anybody at this college. It's not what you'd call an ideal teaching environment."

Penny could see now why he made Sammie so angry. "It depends," she said, as she shifted her backpack over her shoulders.

"Depends?"

"On the teacher. I've got to go."

~

Obie Warren was smiling broadly when he strode into room 407 at 10:00 a.m., as Penny was setting her backpack on the desk to unload her books and papers. His eyes spoke his happiness. Funny how much eyes could tell you. Obie was so easy. He and she simply connected. It was all in the eyes. It went back to their conversation one Sunday morning during that very tense election when Rick was running for county commissioner three years earlier, and Penny had been visiting Cathy's Sunday school class. They had talked of what it was to hear a call, as Isaiah had, and Penny had admitted, though not a church-goer, that she lived with that sense of being called. Now it was true, she realized, that she had felt called to come teach at St. Francis. It had felt right, even if the students were being jerks in the short run and Oscar was overdoing his use of her as confidante. She hadn't been to the office yet for her mail. She would go after this class.

At a few minutes after ten, Lashandra and Letitia came in together, and Penny noticed that Letitia now had similarly braided and beaded dreads. There were only eight in the seminar, and Penny moved to make a circle of the chairs with hers in front of her desk. Obie joined in arranging the chairs. Lashandra and Letitia sat down directly opposite Penny and smiled at her. Penny walked over to them as the other students drifted in. "I hadn't realized, Letitia, that Malvina Johnson was your aunt. She's a very good friend of mine."

"Yes, ma'am. She called me last night and said I was lucky to have you."

Penny looked over at Lashandra. "I'm very glad you like writing. How did you do with your autobiography?"

Lashandra looked at Letitia, who said, "Go on, tell her."

"You tol' us to write at least five pages. I started when I was born, August 1, 1980, in Lander, South Carolina, and I kept going. I couldn't stop. It was fun to think back and remember everything I could. We live on a farm." She looked down at the notebook on her desk. "Ms. Weaver, I wrote thirty pages last night, and then I had to stay up till one o'clock to do my Pre-Comp homework."

Penny exulted. "That's great, Lashandra. "You must be a writer if you enjoy it that much."

"Yeah," she said, and she looked directly and happily at Penny. "It was fun. I didn't want to stop."

Penny became aware that the murmur of conversation she had been hearing had stopped, and they were all listening. It was time to start the class. She walked back to her chair, sat down and smiled, first at Lashandra, and then at the others. "Creative writing should be fun. How many of you enjoyed starting your autobiography? Good. Now I want to read you a little from the autobiography of one of my favorite authors, Zora Neale Hurston."

Penny picked up *Dust Tracks on the Road* and began at the beginning: "Like the dead-seeming, cold rocks, I have memories ..."

~

Her Creative Writing class had been a peaceful interlude. She was surprised when Obie looked at his watch. She glanced at hers, saw it was nearly 11:20, and

Lashandra was still in full spate. She waited for her to pause and then said gently, "It's past time, Lashandra. I hope I haven't made any of you late for your next class. I really enjoyed your writing today. For next Tuesday, keep going. You can turn in what you have now, but add more to it, and turn it all in by Tuesday. Have a good weekend."

She stood and watched them file out, Lashandra whispering to Letitia and seeming reluctant to leave, then whispering to Penny as she walked by, "Thank you, Ms. Weaver."

"Keep it up, Lashandra," she said. "You're a good writer. Spend ten or fifteen minutes a day reading if you want to be even better."

Lashandra stopped, looked at Penny intently, then turned to go, half-dancing out into the hall. Penny was surprised to see Ronny of the balloon muscles stick his head in the door.

"Ms. Weaver, can I ast you somethin'?"

She beckoned, and he came in. Obie had finished putting the chairs back as they had been and now noticed Ronny. He glanced at Penny, who smiled. "Thanks, Obie."

"Hi, Coach," said Ronny. "I had a question 'bout my English homework."

"You came to the right place then, Ronny. I'll see you after lunch for our meeting."

He waved to Penny and walked with a spring in his step out into the hall.

Penny turned to Ronny. She remembered that he hadn't turned in his homework at the end of the eight o'clock class. Now he paged through a worn composition book. "This here, Miz Weaver. I ain't understood this here part."

She looked. He'd written down the questions, painstakingly copied. He had the handwriting of a much younger person.

"Where's your book, Ronny?"

"I ain't got mine yet. My money done run out. Terence let me copy the questions from his book. Is this here the right answer?"

"You need a book, Ronny. Talk to Coach Warren about it. You've got the wrong questions. These are from Chapter Two. Your homework was to answer the questions at the end of Chapter One."

"But, Miz Weaver--"

"Ronny, go talk to Coach Warren. I will help you, but first you must have a book, then read and study it before you try to answer the questions."

Despite being so pumped, Ronny's shoulders sagged. "Okay." He did not sound okay. He turned to go, walking slowly and awkwardly off, clutching his battered composition book.

Penny was turning to gather her things when someone else stuck his head around the door. "Derek, what are you doing here?"

Four

Thursday, February 15. "Have you got a minute, Penny?" Derek Hargrave glanced around the empty classroom. When he looked back at her, she knew something was up. He was wearing his "all business" look, and his brown eyes looked worried.

"Has something happened to Sammie?" What else would bring Derek to the campus during his working hours?

"No, Sammie's fine, far as I know. I'm here on an investigation. Can we talk in here?"

Penny turned and led the way back to her desk, set down her backpack and took the desk chair while he closed the door. "I don't think there are any classes in here until noon. But I have my office hours now. I'm supposed to be next door in the Writing Center."

Derek took a student desk on the front row, held her eyes, and stroked his mustache. He was a dear friend, but if this was a new case, which his stiff body language suggested, why did he want to talk to her here? The college was in Wake County; Shagbark was his jurisdiction.

"I won't keep you but a minute. There's been a tragic death here, Penny, your Provost."

"Audrey White?" She immediately thought of Oscar and his tale of losing it with Audrey. Uh, oh.

"Yes, she was murdered in her home last night. We've taken her husband into custody, but we're investigating here, too, working with the Wake County officers. She lives in The Hills of the Haw, where she was found, so technically she's ours."

Oscar had been so angry, but surely he wouldn't have come to Penny to fuss like he had that morning if he had killed the woman. She suddenly felt protective of her new boss. She had sensed that his rage was mainly for dramatic effect, along the lines of "hit the mule over the head to get its attention," but she didn't know him that well, and how could she help Derek anyway? This was only her second day of teaching at this college.

"I need you to be my eyes and ears," said Derek. "I can't get these people to open up. I've just come from your chairman, Oscar Ferrell. He must know more than he's saying, but it's like prying a bone away from a hungry dog. I can't get him to tell me anything. I can't get through."

Join the club, thought Penny. Derek hardly ever asked for her help even though she had often solved his cases before he did. His normal mode was to tell her to keep out of his investigation. She didn't want to be his eyes and ears here. In any case, if she told him about Oscar's real feelings about the Provost, she would be betraying a confidence. She hadn't wanted the confidence in the first place, but having this knowledge now, she wasn't about to throw Oscar to the wolves, even if one of the wolves was her dear friend Derek.

"Oscar's very honest," she said. "I'm sure he'll help you if he can. He's that kind of person. He's been very helpful to me. Sammie and Malvina admire him. The college is lucky to have him. He's Rick's friend, too, you know, and Rick has known him much longer than I have."

Derek got up and began walking back and forth in front of her, smoothing his mustache. "I know all that," he said, "but the point is, Penny, when I talked to the Provost's secretary not long ago, she said Oscar had been in her office yesterday afternoon shouting at Dr. White that she was letting the college go down the tubes, that the President was an academic disgrace, and so was she if she couldn't run things better. According to the secretary, Ferrell was out for blood. She heard him say, 'It's you or me, and it won't be me who pays for this.' Then he stormed out."

Talk about divided loyalty. Penny watched him stride back and forth, then stop and look at her for some answer.

"I see your problem," she said, "but Oscar's no killer. I do know that much. He's a crusader, trying to bring this college up, to save it. It's on the edge of not surviving. I grant you, Oscar's passionate, but I've only been here since Tuesday, Derek. The whole thing sounds very complicated. How can I possibly help?"

Derek came and stood right in front of the desk. "Listen and observe, Penny. You know people talk to you and trust you. They may talk to you when they clam up for me. Then tell me your thoughts. Is that too much to ask?"

Yes, she thought, definitely too much. "I had only briefly met Audrey White last Monday when Oscar hired me. You know I'm at the bottom of the totem pole here, Derek. I'm a lowly, brand new adjunct. These power struggles that involve the Provost and the President–how could I possibly have any understanding of what's happening at that level?"

"Penny." He leaned across the desk, his hands on it. "You're evading the issue. Will you help me by listening, by noticing things? Usually you're dying to help me, Penny. What's going on? What's the problem? Somebody killed an important figure in the black community here. Don't you want justice?"

That felt below the belt, but she had to admit that it was a fair question. She always wanted justice, but this all was looking very murky to her. Besides that, she tried to listen to herself, to her own conscience. Where had she best be standing in this situation when, whichever way she went, she'd hurt someone she loved and valued. So there it was. She did love Oscar, even if it made not one whit of sense. How in the world had she gotten herself into this predicament?

It was true that she was back-pedaling on this one. She could see how it must look to Derek. Face it, she told herself, you're terrified you'll betray Oscar, for that's what it would be if she broke his confidence.

She looked up at Derek. He was begging her with his eyes, and she had known and cared about him a long time, nearly ten years. She usually loved helping him. Goddess, this was too hard.

"Okay, Derek, as long as you understand that I'm brand new here, still getting my land legs. Don't assume my perspective will be helpful." She turned, stared out the window. Another beautiful February day of blue sky and bright sun.

There was a knock at the door. It was Oscar, his face briefly at the window, then gone. He was looking for her. "I have to get to my office hours, Derek. I'll try. That's the best I can offer."

His shoulders relaxed. He hadn't seen Oscar's face through the door's window. "I'll call you at home tonight then. Thanks, Penny. I knew you'd do it."

Oscar had disappeared by the time she and Derek left the classroom, and it was already 11:40. She was way late for her office hours. Derek being on her heels, she decided to go on to the Writing Center. She might have students waiting. She could find Oscar later, or he would find her. He knew where she was supposed to be.

No students came to consult her. She read the homework papers she had collected that morning, then went to Oscar's office. She didn't want to hear his version of his interview with Derek, but he would probably tell her. She wished she could go home for the day, but she was riding back with Sammie at three. She could at least escape to the library once she'd checked in with Oscar. He might have wanted to talk to her about something else entirely. Fat chance, she thought. He had already had the Provost on his mind. Now he would for sure.

As soon as she entered the English Department office and went to her box to get any memos–nothing today, Oscar popped out of his office and beckoned to her. "Are you free for a minute?"

"For a minute. I'm starving. I need to go eat lunch." She walked in, sat down in the chair nearest the door, and he immediately shut it behind her and turned the lock. "Why was that policeman talking to you? He doesn't think you killed Audrey, does he?"

Here we go, she thought. Talk about walking the edge of a precipice. "He's a friend. Derek Hargrave is Sammie Hargrave's husband. You know, I mentioned that he worked for the Shagbark County Sheriff's Department when we were talking this morning. He knew I worked here now and stopped to say hello."

Not quite the whole story. Athena, may I be wise.

Oscar was pacing in front of his bookshelves. "Your friend came in to talk to me. He practically accused *me* of killing Audrey. The man's incompetent, a jerk. Obviously he isn't used to being around academics."

"Oscar, he's married to an academic, Sammie. He's quite competent. I know him well, know his integrity. He's trying to find out what happened, that's all. It's his job."

"Then he's going about it all wrong. Is he going to use you as a spy?"

She felt like he'd landed a punch in her solar plexus. She caught her breath. Talk about being intuitive. Bull's eye. She owed him at least some of the truth. "He does want my general impressions. I don't call that spying," though spying was exactly what Derek was asking of her. She wasn't going to do it if she could help it. Oh, Athena! "I told him I was brand new two days ago, a mere adjunct, that I didn't know the players."

"Does he think I killed her?"

"At this point he's trying to get the lay of the land, that's all, as far as I can tell. He has arrested her husband, he said." Should she tell him she'd insisted to Derek that Oscar was not a killer? No, best not to get into that at all. He would know then that they had talked about him.

"That idiot? He's too drunk to kill anybody. Besides, he adored Audrey. I don't know how she tolerated him. She told me he was falling down drunk every night." He shook his head and sat down behind his desk. "As you know, I disagreed with Audrey yesterday. That prissy secretary told your friend," he said with heavy sarcasm, "that I was shouting at Audrey. I was. I get so angry sometimes. I know it doesn't do any good. You've got to sweet talk these women at the top to get anywhere. I keep forgetting. But Penny, I didn't kill her. Why would I do that? I don't kill people to make my point. They simply want to get rid of me here. Siler would love to have me arrested. I'm a thorn in her flesh."

There was open anguish in his eyes when he looked up. "All I wanted was for Audrey to help me get that bastard Clarkson fired. It's outrageous what he's doing to these naive young women, these children. Lord, help me. I should have stayed away from this college, all these failing HBCUs. I'm not cut out for fights like this."

Penny surprised herself by saying, "Actually, you are. Who but someone who wants to make this college better, help these students achieve something, should be in this fight? You know it's a fight and a worthy one. It's hard is all."

"Oh, Penny, you have no idea. It's more than hard. The President is out to crucify me. I've upset her apple cart, and she doesn't give a damn about the college. It's her get rich quick scheme. I could swear that she and that Finance Officer Grubb are cooking the books."

He broke off, got up, and began pacing again. Then he stopped in front of her and gave her a searching look. "It does help so much to talk to you, Penny. I trust you. Am I wrong to trust you? I don't ordinarily trust white people, as I told you, but for some reason I can't fathom I do trust you. I feel like I can say anything to you, and you'll understand. Am I wrong?"

She found herself saying, "Yes, you can trust me. I'll keep your counsel. As far as understanding what you tell me, I'll do my best. But I'm starving, Oscar." She lightened her voice. "I need to go eat lunch."

She stood up, but before she could pick up her back pack, he had his arms around her. He hugged her tight and kissed her cheek. "Thank you, Penny. You're amazing. I don't know, one of a kind."

"At the moment hungry," she said and smiled into his eyes. Let me out of here, she thought, before he kisses me again.

~

Penny had stopped to use the bathroom and was waiting by the fourth floor elevator when she heard shouting. Oscar. "You are offensive, sir, contemptible. Get out and stay out. If I were the President of this college, I'd fire you so fast, your head would spin."

At that moment the elevator door opened, and a very elegantly dressed and coifed light-skinned black woman stepped out. Despite every hair being in place, she looked like a pig on its hind legs. She was short and pudgy, but she carried herself as if convinced of her own importance. She hurried off, her spike heels clicking, in the direction of Oscar's office. Penny was so fascinated, she forgot to get on the elevator. Its doors closed, and it disappeared. She punched "down" again. You never knew with this elevator where it was because the floor indicator lights were broken. It could come right back, or it could take some time, even get stuck on another floor. She could have taken the stairs, but she waited. No more shouting. She did hear a door slam. Oscar's probably.

Then the elegant woman reappeared, walking with Clarkson. He took one long, slow stride to three of the woman's short, fast ones, and he was walking bent over in order to hear her. They made a strange pair. In most situations he would have been the one at ease, the authority figure, but here he seemed very determined to catch her every word, as though each one mattered a great deal to him at this moment. The elevator returned as they walked up.

As Penny got on, she heard the woman say, "Don't worry about it, Ed. You're one of our few tenured faculty. He doesn't even have a contract."

She had preceded him onto the elevator, stood by the panel of buttons facing the door, as if Penny weren't even there, and pushed the one for the first floor.

Clarkson said, "Three for me." He nodded to acknowledge Penny, then ignored her.

"No, Ed. We need to talk. Let's go to my office. We'll be private. I'll order us some sandwiches."

"Thanks, Christine. I'm sorry to add anything to your burden. This must be one hell of a day for you with Audrey dead."

Then Penny knew who the woman must be: Christine Siler, the President. She certainly seemed very chummy with this History professor whom Oscar and Sammie hated. No wonder Oscar had been shouting. Clarkson, however, was apparently in no danger of being fired by the college President.

~

Penny had finished marking all the homework papers that had been turned in (not many) and had sketched out her next Tuesday's lesson plans. She was packing up to go meet Sammie when someone put his hands over her eyes. Only one person did that to her. She lifted Kenneth's hands and turned. "You? Here? Sammie's giving me a ride. Did you forget?" she whispered.

He kissed her and pulled a chair over close to hers. She had been working in a quiet corner on the third floor of the library. No one else was around. She'd been alone with a photo poster she loved of Zora Neale Hurston laughing.

"I've been hired here," he said quietly.

"To work here, you mean?"

"Yes. Security guard, undercover for Derek. He thinks something's going on over here that's related to your Provost's murder. He thinks you and I will sort it out, wants us both on the scene." His eyes were warm and full of love. She was glad that he now worked part-time for the Shagbark County Sheriff's Department, but was it wise of Derek to have him here?

Whatever other feelings she sometimes had, there was no one in the world like Kenneth. Thank the goddesses they'd found each other. "Yes, he told me to let him know what I observed, but it's uncomfortable, being a spy like this. What could I possibly learn when I'm so new, so unimportant to the higher-ups here?"

Even as she said it, she knew she wasn't being straight with him. She already knew far too much about the higher-ups, thanks to Oscar.

He grinned at her. "Oh, I don't know, Penny. When I first met you, you'd only been on Gower a few days, but you already knew a lot about the guests in your B and B, whom you'd met a day or so before. People talk to you. You'll have it all sorted out in no time."

She stood up. "Hardly. But you'll be in the thick of it, I bet. There are drugs all over the place here, but you know that. How did you get hired so fast?"

"Derek was determined, took me to President Siler's office, and insisted. She was close to Audrey White. She gave in. She wants the killer found. She's scared, said so. Derek persuaded her that I was the ticket."

"You're the ticket, all right," said Penny. He grabbed her and hugged her tight.

"Now look, Kenneth. I need to catch my ride back with Sammie. You're staying longer?"

"Yes, all evening until the kids are settled in for the night. I get off at eleven. Go catch Sammie. We'll talk more when I get home." He squeezed her again and kissed her gently on the lips. "You're a love." Then they headed for the stairs.

Five

Thursday, February 15. "That's some scary, the Provost getting herself killed," Obie said as Sammie was accelerating onto I-40. That Thursday afternoon Obie had hitched a ride back to Riverdell with Sammie and Penny. His car was in the shop. He had insisted that Penny sit in front, but he was leaning over the front seat.

"I wonder who she riled this time," said Sammie. "She was not my favorite person, always behind the scenes. You never knew where you were. Smart, but using it to fool people. She had to have everybody in their place. Even a black college can be run like a plantation if the people at the top think they're Massa and the Overseer."

Penny laughed. "She was the overseer?" She visualized Audrey White, slender, not much over five feet, light skin, grey eyes, straightened hair, looking very chic. She hadn't seemed powerful to her, despite the power suit and heels she wore, but neither had the pig-shaped President whom Clarkson had clearly thought was powerful enough to warrant the trouble of buttering her up. True, Oscar had been furious about White's misuse of power. Penny had never been good at respecting pecking orders. She liked to level the field, not make stepping stones for some to use to look down on their fellows.

"She wasn't so bad," said Obie. "She was very nice to me when I got hired. She and Coach Cox took me out to celebrate to a very high class restaurant."

"That's because the football team is supposed to bring in alumni dollars to dig them out of the red. They didn't take me or Penny out to dinner."

"I'm only Assistant Coach," said Obie. "I can't hardly bring the team up by myself. It'll take years to get these boys in shape, if Coach Cox can do it. He not very energetic."

"You can say that again," said Sammie. Once more she had kicked off her heels, lime green today to go with her lime green suit and earrings. "He's a three-toed sloth. No wonder those boys do drugs and rape girls. He's not got them under a tight discipline. But you'll help, Obie. If anybody can get those boys in hand, you can."

Obie was quiet. He looked embarrassed. "I try."

"We all try," said Sammie, "but help at the top could make a hell of a big difference."

"That's what frustrates Oscar, too," Penny said. Then she wondered if she'd said too much. Maybe Sammie would tell Derek that Oscar talked to Penny. In fact, maybe she already had. She couldn't remember exactly what she'd said to her about Oscar.

"Oscar's in hot water now, since Audrey died," said Sammie. "Word is he had a huge knock-down, drag-out fight with her the afternoon before she was killed. You hear about that, Penny?"

"Derek told me. I said Oscar's not the type to kill. He is passionate, all right."

"He threw Terence out of his class for sleeping 'bout a week ago," Obie said. "Terence was hot, but I've felt like throwing Terence off the team once or twice myself. Terence is tough. Sweet talk runs off him."

Sammie snorted and swerved around a car going the speed limit. "You betcha," she said, "but stuff like that and raising cane with the Provost won't win him any brownie points with the Prez."

Penny wanted to say, "He doesn't want brownie points. He wants to make the college better," but she decided to wait. The whole thing was so tricky now. She was trying hard not to violate Oscar's confidences.

"Then it turned out Terence was in the wrong class anyway. You have him now, right, Miss Penny?"

"I do."

"How he doin'?"

"He has a book. That's a start, but he and Ronny both did the wrong homework. Chapter Two instead of Chapter One, and they had the exact same answers."

"Uh-oh," said Obie. "I'll speak to them about it."

"I will, too," said Penny, "when I give the papers back. All your freshman players do seem to be trying. They don't all have books though. Can you do anything about that?"

"I can try," said Obie. "You notice the clothes they wear? The gold chains? Terence's outfit probably cost him five hundred dollars, that watch alone maybe a thousand, and he's not the only one. They spend all their money on clothes, girls, Walkmans and CDs. They don't buy books. They brag about that."

"Work on them, Obie," said Sammie. "That's ridiculous, if they want to pass college."

"Oh, Sammie," said Penny, "I was going to tell you. Oscar said he wants to do a women's studies seminar next term, history and literature. He wants to work on it with you."

"You're serious, girl?"

"I am."

"Whoopee. Now if we can get it approved by the Provost. Oops, no Provost. Who will take her place, do you think? I hope to hell it's not Clarkson."

~

Penny came bolt awake. What had roused her? When she turned on the bedside lamp, she heard an owl hooting. Oh, the new bird clock. Midnight already. She could hear the clock's gentle tick, tick once the owl was quiet. It was quiet in the neighborhood, too. It must be time for Kenneth to get home. Then she heard a car. Yes, it was their old Dodge, still running. If cars could be faithful, Athena was, eighteen years old and still flying along. Thank you, Athena.

The engine cut off, and the door shut. She felt with her feet for her slippers. She wanted to hear how his first shift had gone. He'd learned a lot about American ways since they married in 1992, but the black college with its large number of inner city kids would be a whole new challenge. He was good with people. He'd make it work for him. Exactly how he would do it was an interesting question.

She opened the door just as he was inserting the key in the lock.

"Hi, love. You're still awake?"

She reached to hug him as he closed the door behind him and secured the lock. Then he held her tightly. "We have any milk? I could use a milky drink. I'm exhausted but wide awake. And you? Would you keep me company, compare notes? You up for that, love?"

"Of course." She walked over to the stove. "Ovaltine or cocoa?"

"You choose."

"Ovaltine, then. I'm so glad we can still get it in the U.K. and bring some back with us. I never get tired of it. Childhood comfort food, I guess."

She poured two cups of milk into a saucepan and put the heat on medium high. She'd stir it to keep it from scorching. "How did it go tonight?"

He'd stripped off his jacket, slacks, shirt, and was tying the belt of his robe. "Good, I think. I ended up in a bull session in the football dorm."

"Sounds good. You moved fast. They must like you."

"I liked them more than I expected to. I met some of your students. I believe you have a Ronny and a Terence?"

"Oh, yes. What did you learn? I'd love to know more about those two, some of my potential troublemakers."

"They didn't give me any trouble, but I did have to chase Merilee out of Ronny's room. Girls are supposed to leave the boys' dorm by nine, and this was after ten. Her counselor called me, worried about her. I escorted her back and then returned to check the dorm for any other females, as these lads refer to women. Thanks, Penny."

She handed him a mug and set a plate of digestive biscuits between them, sat down at the other end of their couch, and tucked her feet up. "But you stayed?"

"I came back. I'm supposed to go the rounds, check that the main buildings are secure, make sure there are no students wandering around after ten, but they invited me back, so I went. I could have sat in the guard shack, but they issued me a cell phone and a beeper. I thought getting to know these blokes might help Derek. They know things and have opinions I could pass on."

Penny sipped her drink. Exactly the right hotness. "What on earth did you talk about?"

"Sex and females."

"Kenneth."

"They were very interested to learn I was your husband. I told them you were very hot in bed."

She punched his arm, and his drink sloshed. "You didn't?"

He laughed deeply and happily, wiped at his robe. "Of course not. They asked me that, and I said you had a mean temper, and if they wanted to pass your course, they'd better spend a lot of time with their books and not get distracted by females."

"I hope they take your advice, but from what I've seen so far, it would be a miracle if Terence and Ronny pass this course."

"They like you," he said. "They were agog about my being married to you. 'What's she like, Mr. Morgan?' I said, 'She's mean as a snake. I have to do exactly what she orders me to do.'"

"Brother. I'll never live down this reputation you're building up for me."

"I've got them worried, Penny. They'll behave better now." He set his cup down on the floor. "Come hither, love. I've missed you."

She snuggled against him. "Tell me what else they talked about."

"Mostly about you, a good sign. You've made a big impression already. They were worried about their grades even before we talked."

"That's a good sign?"

"Oh, yes. These blokes have so many other things on their minds."

"Females and drugs?"

"So cynical you are, Penny." He hugged her. "Terence talked about his three children."

"He has children?" She pictured this young man with the gold teeth and cocaine habit, who had so infuriated Oscar, and with whom she was already battling wits.

"Three, ages three and under. They're in Camden. He's not married to their mother, but he supports them all. He's very proud of his children, Penny. He said, and I quote, 'I want my boy baby to grow up to be a hell-raiser like me.'"

"Oh, wow. He supports them with his drug money?"

"He didn't say that, but he did say he has two younger brothers who work for him and take care of business while he's here. His mother's in prison. He never knew his father. It's hard for me to conceive such a life, but here he is in college. He wants that degree, and I sense his intelligence. Whether he'll settle down and work, I have no idea, but if anyone can get him to do that, you can, love."

"You, too, Obie. The men as models may be more crucial."

"Maybe, maybe not. He must have had a strong mother to cope as well as he has. It's a lifestyle so foreign to me, but I like him. We connected, to my surprise. He's a good bloke, Penny, underneath."

"But tough, remember." She yawned.

"Yes, tough on the outside, but soft on the inside. Your chairman throwing him out in the hall in front of his classmates was quite offensive to him. He hates Oscar Ferrell. So does Ronny. They called him a prick, that lovely American term I've adopted. I think they may be right." He was watching her face, lifting an eyebrow. "Oscar is black, so maybe he gets away with it, but I don't think it was a clever move, if he cares to educate Terence, and Terence is very intelligent, even if his education is lacking."

"I agree to the intelligence, but I think Oscar has an instinct for what will work in a given situation." She yawned again. "Let's to bed, love."

"No, wait. This is important. Oscar Ferrell lost Terence's trust when he manhandled him. He hurt his pride, and underneath his ego is still raw from it. He's easy to hurt."

"I don't agree," said Penny. "Of course, I wouldn't get physical with my students."

"I would certainly hope not." Kenneth was angry now.

"But I think Oscar senses that such a strategy will get Terence's attention so he will take college seriously and buckle down to work."

"Wait, love. You admire Oscar for throwing a twenty-two-year old out of his classroom? Do you also think it was clever for him to scream at the Provost when he was angry at how she was handling things? Is that the mark of an adult, Penny? The man is childish. He's losing his temper when people don't respond well to him. Why don't you see that?"

She felt like she was sliding down a steep embankment and couldn't see the bottom. He was jealous. He had reason to be, which she couldn't admit to him, but she couldn't let him run down Oscar either. "He's dramatic, Kenneth, that's all. The kids get it, even if you don't. The Provost probably wasn't that upset either."

"We'll never know. She's dead now, and he's a suspect." He stood up, grabbed their mugs, and carried them to the sink. He ran water in them. He wasn't looking at her, and his back was stiff.

She hated it when they clashed. Normally, they were so peaceful together, so easy, so trusting. He was part of herself. But now, working at the college, both in new territory, feeling their way, it was harder. She'd have to help him understand Oscar better. She didn't understand everything, but Oscar's whole behavior, even the things that he himself felt bad about, made sense to her. He could be outrageous, yes, but that somehow fitted the situation. But Kenneth didn't want her thoughts now.

"Why do you admire that kind of behavior, Penny? It's sick; it's infantile. If I acted like that, you'd leave me." She wanted to argue so much. It hurt that he couldn't see Oscar and his rages as she did. They were honest. They matched the horribly unfair odds that were so stacked against anything in the college working right. But it was late, after 1:00 a.m. They were both exhausted, and she ached with worry for Oscar. Then fighting with Kenneth was so depressing. Anything she could say to defend Oscar would further inflame him, so all she said was, "I'd never leave you." She hoped that was true. She wanted it to be true.

Saturday morning, Penny woke to the sound of a power mower outside the window. Andy next door must be mowing. No, wait. It was February. She looked at the clock. Nearly 9:00 a.m. She'd really slept. Kenneth was up and gone. She pulled on her robe, stepped into her slippers, and walked to the window. No, Andy was tilling his garden, taking advantage of what looked to be another spring day. February weather was unpredictable in North Carolina, but she knew from other springs that Andy liked to start his onions, peas, lettuce, beets and cabbages early.

When someone knocked at the door and tried the handle, she opened it to her daughter Sarah, holding little Seb, who struggled to get free of her arms while saying, "Down, down."

"Can I talk to you a minute, Mom?"

"Sure. Hi, Seb." Penny looked around. Seb was two and heavily into investigating cupboards, climbing onto the toilet tank, throwing things to see if they broke. "You can let him down. I think we're baby proofed. Ah, Kenneth made coffee. Want some?"

"I'd love some. Can I have some of your bread, too?"

Seb had made a beeline for the bathroom. "Help yourself, Sarah. I need to pee and comb my hair. I'll check that he can't hurt himself or anything else in the bathroom."

"You go. I'll give him some bread and honey. Then shut the bathroom door. It's easier." Sarah grabbed Seb and a telephone book and sat him in a kitchen chair. "Honey, Seb?"

"Honey." He nodded vigorously.

"What's up?" said Penny when she'd sat down at the table with her grandson. The baby was doing so beautifully. Sarah was bringing him up on her own. His father, Penny's neighbor Leroy, babysat him a lot, but Sarah hadn't wanted to marry Leroy. It was an unusual arrangement, but to Penny's relief, it was working. "He's really grown since last October. Talking a lot, too. You're doing a great job, Sarah."

"I guess." Sarah handed Seb some small pieces of bread, butter and honey and sat down opposite Penny, after putting a big plate of bread, butter, and honey between them but out of Seb's reach. He was eyeing it as he stuffed his bread and honey into his mouth. He uttered a muffled, "More" and pounded the table.

"Oh, I forgot the coffee." Sarah jumped up, grabbed the pot, the milk she'd already set out, and two mugs. "Mom, I've got a big problem. Seb, chew what's in your mouth first." Seb continued pounding, but apparently he understood.

"What's the problem?"

"I'm dating somebody, and he doesn't like Leroy. He thinks he's weird."

"Leroy is weird," Penny said. "Years ago we all worried about Leroy, his shaved head, his strange ways, but we learned to trust him, right? You trusted him enough to have his baby. Has that changed? Leroy loves Seb, and he has helped you a lot with babysitting."

"No, I think he's a good part-time father, you know. I'm not saying that, but Brian wants us to live together, and he doesn't think it's good for Seb to be around Leroy."

All Penny could think of was how Leroy doted on this child, his blond hair sticking straight up, his mouth smeared with honey, his pudgy arms reaching for the bread and butter plate. Sarah was distracted, watching Penny for her reaction. Penny broke off a piece of bread and gave it to Seb. Sarah had let Leroy and Seb learn to love each other. That bond was surely important to save, but she knew that Sarah, even when she asked for advice, rarely wanted to hear anything that Penny suggested. Half the time she'd already made up her mind. "What do you think?"

"I mean, Leroy has helped me a lot, and he and Seb get along, but wouldn't it be better for Seb to be around a man who's normal?"

It would be so tragic for Leroy if Sarah withdrew Seb. "Wouldn't it be possible for Seb to have time with both men?"

"Not if Brian hates it. He'd bug me all the time."

"Maybe if he saw how good Leroy is with Seb, it would reassure him. How well does he know Leroy?"

"He doesn't know him at all. I mean, he has been with me a few times when I came to pick up Seb. Leroy has kept him when we've had dates."

"Who will keep him when you two need to go out if you don't use Leroy?"

"Maybe you, when you're here, or Belle and Kate. They love having him around. He calls them both Grandma."

Penny had to remind herself that her landladies knew her grandson better than she did. Sometimes, briefly, she regretted their double country lifestyle, half a year in Wales, half a year in North Carolina, but Sarah was avoiding the issue. "Have you talked to Leroy about it?"

"Of course not. It's why I'm talking to you, Mom. You're not being helpful."

"I do think Leroy is good for Seb, and Seb is good for Leroy. I doubt Leroy will make Seb weird. After all, I'm rather weird myself, and he's my grandson."

Sarah pushed back her chair. "I gotta go, Mom. C'mon, Seb. Outside?"

Seb, his face and hands sticky, his cheeks bulging, put up his arms. Sarah scooped him up. "See you later, Mom." She grabbed a sponge off the counter, quickly wiped Seb's hands and face, and slammed out the door.

Six

Saturday, February 17. Penny dressed slowly. The scene with Sarah had depressed her. She wanted the best possible life for little Seb and for Sarah, too. Sarah was now bent on making herself a nuclear family, even though Penny had thought her perfectly happy as an independent single mom, earning her living and having the support of the baby's father and all their good friends here when she and Kenneth were in Wales.

This re-entry was not unlike others she'd had after being away for months. She usually came back to a multiplicity of problems and crises. She surely had a fistful of them now. She felt like going back to bed. What was she going to do about Oscar?

She finished pinning up her braid and walked to the telephone. She'd call Cathy. She always felt better after they talked things over, but no one answered at the Cleggs'. She left a message to call when convenient. She and Kenneth would be home all day, though outside some.

Then she tied on her old gardening shoes, picked up her gloves, and went down to see if she could help Andy. She found him, Kenneth and Leroy consulting about which seeds to plant in which rows. They were standing near the silent rototiller, drinking coffee. Sarah's car was gone. Andy's and Jan's twins, Penny and Kenny, were picking up stones in the tilled area and putting them in a rusty wheelbarrow. Little Seb had been enlisted, too, and was following the lead of the twins, who would be seven in April. Penny had had a hand in their being in the world at all, since their mother had had to make a tough decision when she discovered that she was pregnant during her senior year of high school.

She missed seeing these little ones, too, godchildren to her and Kenneth, and their namesakes. They were already in first grade, bright, active, happy children. They were good for Seb, too. She stood a moment at the edge of the tilled area watching Seb try to lift a stone too big for his small hands. It kept slipping out. Little Penny came over to him. "I'll get that one, Seb."

"No! Me do it," he cried.

She wisely pointed to several smaller ones. "You get those, Seb. I'll get this big one," and he hurried to get the smaller ones and threw them with enthusiasm into the wheelbarrow. They clanged and banged against the other rocks, and he laughed and looked for more stones he could hurl. Then little Penny noticed her watching and came running to her.

"Aunt Penny, we're making the garden. Want to help us?" She threw her arms around Penny, who'd bent to hug her. Penny held up her gardening gloves. "Put me to work."

Little Penny tugged her over to where the men were. "What can I do?" Penny asked.

Andy smiled. "It's so good to have you guys back in the neighborhood. We've been consulting. I believe we'll do the sugar snap peas along the back fence, then the beets, then the onions, then the cabbages, carrots, lettuce, and radishes closest to the house. The soil is looser up close here." He looked out at his tilling. "I see a few more stones, Pen and Ken. Can you get them? And watch Seb. He's throwing the stones out of the wheelbarrow back into the garden."

Kenny, his red hair flopping, made a dash for Seb, who had been left alone with the wheelbarrow full of rocks and was happily throwing them in the wrong direction. Little Penny had run over, too, and said, "Look, Seb. Let's pick them up and throw them back again. We don't want ugly rocks in the garden. We want the veggies to grow here."

"Me like rocks," Seb said and threw another one out.

"Look, Seb," said Kenny. "Here's one. Throw it back into the wheelbarrow," and he demonstrated with a loud, clanging toss. Seb found one to clang into the barrow, too. While he was occupied with returning the rocks to their planned destination, the twins ran around the garden area looking for rocks they'd missed.

"Who wants to plant peas?" asked Andy, as he shifted the wheelbarrow while Leroy scooped up Seb.

"Me! Me!" shouted the twins, and Seb echoed, "Me, me!"

"Seb, you and I can plant onions," said Leroy. He picked up the paper bag of onion sets. Andy turned on the tiller and ran it once again to create the rows about eighteen inches apart. Penny and Kenny knew the routine and waited at either end of the pea row until he'd cut a furrow, and then on hands and knees, they moved along, putting a pea every inch or so until they met in the middle. Then they turned and went back the way they'd come, smoothing soil over the seeds, and patting it down.

Meantime Kenneth was seeding the beets, Leroy and Seb were pushing the onion sets into the third row, and Penny planted the cabbage seedlings. Last, when he'd turned off the tiller, Andy started down the carrot row, also on his hands and knees. While he did the lettuce plants, Kenneth did the radishes.

Penny had finished her cabbage plants when Belle and Kate emerged from the big house to which Penny and Kenneth's garage apartment was attached. They each had a coffee mug in hand and came over to inspect the garden. "Isn't it too early, Andy?" asked Belle, his mother-in-law. "It's lovely today, but we could have a blizzard tomorrow."

"It's okay, Mom." Andy looked up from his planting. "This is a spring garden, and these peas, beets and stuff can take frost. I'll cover the lettuces if it freezes. I've got a roll of remay, in case. It's tomatoes and peppers, the summer garden crops, that you wait to plant until there won't be more frost. These babies like the cold."

Belle, in her sloppy tee and cut offs, her tangled, dark curls reflecting something of her unruly spirit, said, "If you say so," and sat down at the cement picnic table on the patio behind their back door. Kate had walked over to see how the children's planting was going. As usual with Kate, every hair was in place, her shorts and pullover clean and wrinkle free. She squatted to watch Seb push a small onion bulb into the soft soil. "Looks like fun, Seb." She grinned at Leroy.

Seb looked up at her. "G'ma, me plant 'nuns."

"I can see that," Kate said. "Good work, Seb."

"These are too close together, Seb," said Leroy. "Put this one over here," which Seb obediently did.

It hurt Penny to watch. How could Sarah do anything to hurt this father-son bond? She turned away and walked over to sit down by Belle.

"Good to be back, but I'm up to my ears in problems in less than a week," Penny said.

"Tell Grandma," said Belle. "Want some coffee? We've made a fresh pot."

"Sure," said Penny. "Let me go wash my hands."

"Oh, come on in the house, Penny. Wash 'em at our sink. We can talk in the living room. Everyone else is outside. I've been wanting to hear your take on the murder at St. Francis. The Provost, egad. What next?"

When they'd settled in the living room of the house where Penny had once rented a room and heated it from the woodstove in this very room, Penny wondered how much to tell Belle. She was a dear friend, if unpredictable in her enthusiasms and rages, but she could use someone to bounce off of some of the many dilemmas she was revolving in her own mind. Sad to say, she would normally have confided in Kenneth, but something held her back, probably because she knew all too well how he'd react to all of it. Another woman's perspective might help. Belle could be counted on to be honest, and Penny knew Belle loved her, treasured her daughter Sarah, to whom she'd been a second mother, and doted on little Seb. Belle had been and still was a fierce mother to her own daughters, Jan and Wendy, but little Penny, Kenny, and Seb she spoiled every chance she got, feeding them cookies, taking them for ice cream or to buy a toy at the children's shop in the village. "Grandma's privilege," she'd say.

"What's up, Penny? You seem a little down."

"Ah, too much too fast. I like my new job at the college, but it's hard. I think I can do it okay, as far as the teaching. It's all the other stuff."

Belle sipped her coffee. "Other stuff? You mean the murder?"

"Partly, but more than that. I've got basically remedial English with some kids reading and writing at grade school level, the best only at middle school level. My job is to teach them enough so that they can go on to regular Freshman English."

"Sounds hard," said Belle, "but also like something you can do with ease. Penny, it's not like you to complain that something is too hard."

"I know. I can manage the kids, I think, but the chairman, Oscar, whom I like so much, is confiding in me a lot of his problems with the administration, and now there's this murder. Derek wants me to spy on the man, and I can't do that. Oscar is trusting me. I told Derek I'd give him my thoughts on what I learned, only I can't honestly do that, nor can I seem to stop Oscar talking to me about things I don't especially want to know."

"We all love to talk to you, Penny. You see past our funny, awkward ways and love us in spite of ourselves."

"I do?" She looked to see if Belle was serious. It wasn't easy for Belle to admit how important to her other people were, and it was true that Penny had seen the lovable, caring woman Belle was past her rages and temper tantrums.

Belle nodded at her. "You do, Penny. You're one of the few people in my whole life who has understood how I felt underneath all my raging around." She was deadly serious.

Penny had to smile. "Thanks, Belle. That helps. I guess Derek sees something like that. He says people talk to me when they won't talk to him, but I can't tell him everything Oscar tells me. That wouldn't be right. Oscar trusts me to keep his confidences."

"I see why," said Belle. "You're lucky. Your boss likes and trusts you. That should make your work life easy. I don't think I've ever had a boss like that. It's probably the real reason I went independent, when all is said and done. But what about Kenneth? How is he with all this, your new boss and murder where you work, all that. I seem to remember that he has a protective streak."

Penny nodded. Belle was far more astute about her than she'd realized. "At first he was worried about all the sex and drugs on campus. That was before the murder. But, yes, now there's the murder, and Derek has him working there under cover as a security guard. The hardest part, Belle, is that he doesn't like my boss, Oscar."

Belle set her mug down on the floor. "Now I get it. Kenneth is jealous."

"Not yet," said Penny. "He doesn't know how much Oscar has told me and is leaning on me."

"I think he has figured out more than you think, Penny. What do you do when he runs down Oscar?"

Then it hit Penny. Belle was right. She'd been so busy defending Oscar to Kenneth that she'd forgotten that he knew her so well that he had probably figured out that, in spite of her best intentions, she was half in love with Oscar. That would definitely inflame every irrational bone in his body.

~

It wasn't until the following Tuesday morning, when Oscar turned his rage on her, that she began to see him differently. To her relief her eight o'clock class had settled down a lot. Some were still stony faced, a few came late and were locked out, but in the main they were there on time, or at least by ten after, and had their first drafts of their first essay, which had been due that morning. She had let them choose from several topics, among them, the advantages and disadvantages of the single life, a very popular topic among the young men. She was giving them some in-class writing time, reading their drafts and suggesting changes.

When she came to Ronny, still in his place at the back of the room by the window, he handed her his typed sheet. He had the required three paragraphs, but his topic wasn't one of those assigned. Instead he'd chosen to write about "College Extracurricular Activities." The title should have alerted her, but it didn't.

She read it, sitting in a nearby vacant desk, correcting his spelling and punctuation errors automatically. Then the middle paragraph had no errors, which surprised her, nor did the last paragraph, and both read too smoothly for Ronnie's skill level. "Ronny, I can tell that you copied these last two paragraphs. Someone else wrote them. You have to write your own essay. It's okay if you make mistakes. See, you made some here, and I've shown you how to fix them, but you can't copy from other people. That's plagiarism, and I'd have to give you an F. I'll give you a C for now, but I want you to rewrite the whole essay in your own words for Thursday."

"I didn't copy, Miz Weaver. I wrote it all by myself."

"I don't believe you, Ronny. I can tell that most of it is plagiarized. Don't do that again. I don't want to give you Fs. You'll fail this course unless you learn how to write essays. I know you want to graduate. You're here to learn. You can learn to write a good essay."

Ronny shook his head. "It the truth, Miz Weaver. I didn't copy." He didn't look at her. She wrote a C on the paper and gave it back to him. Then she went on to Merilee, who'd heard the whole conversation with Ronny.

Merilee had chosen to write about her hometown, Camden. She had one short paragraph, which Penny could barely read. At least she'd chosen one of the assigned topics, and it was clearly her own effort, but a pitiful effort it was. A second grade child could have done better. "I liv in Camen nu gercy. I liek Camen. I liv wid mama and daddee."

She showed Merilee how to change the spelling, talked with her about details she could add, and encouraged her to type it, if she could, as it was hard to read.

"Yes, ma'am, I will."

"I'll give you a C for this much, Merilee, but for Thursday you need three paragraphs, and your essay should be at least one page long. Penny showed her the page in her book (She had a book.) where this three-paragraph essay was explained and some examples given.

"Thank you, Miz Weaver." She smiled shyly. "I don't want no Fs in your class." Penny thought immediately of Clarkson's offer to give this so vulnerable young woman an A.

"You can learn, Merilee. Keep doing your work." But could Merilee learn? Was it even fair to encourage her when, if she could learn, she probably couldn't learn fast enough?

By the time her Creative Writing Seminar let out at 11:15 a.m. that Tuesday, Penny was exhausted. She listened as patiently as she could to Terence, who'd waited in the hall until all the students had left. He was explaining why he hadn't turned in his first draft. His wife had been in a car accident back in Camden, and he'd been gone over the weekend. Couldn't he have until Thursday? "Please, Miz Weaver. I ain't had no sleep. I had to go home, help my wife. You ain't gonna flunk me for that, is you?"

Not for that, she thought, though with your low reading and writing scores on the placement tests, you haven't much hope, especially if you miss class like this. "One F won't kill you, Terence," she said. "Next time have your essay ready early. You next draft is due Thursday. Be sure that's done on time. You still have forty minutes to get today's draft in if you hurry. Put it in my box by noon."

"But Miz Weaver …"

"I have to go, Terence. I'll see you Thursday."

She slipped her backpack straps over her shoulders and hurried off to the office before any more students delayed her. She was already starving and still had to do her office hours. She'd eaten breakfast at five-thirty. She did need to check her mail in the department office. Then she might get away with eating her peanut butter sandwich and apple covertly in the Writing Center if she had no students seeking her out.

But when she was looking into her box and pulling out two essays, probably from the students she'd locked out, Oscar walked out of his office.

"Ah, Penny, could I talk to you a minute?"

"I have my office hours," she said, but she was thinking of her need to eat soon.

"The students can wait a minute. This won't take long."

She followed him in. She took one of the straight chairs opposite his desk, the one nearest the door, which he closed. Then he settled behind his desk. Was he going to confide in her again something he shouldn't have talked to her about in the first place? She hoped this time his story about the shenanigans the President was up to wasn't too long-winded.

He wanted to talk about something else entirely. "Ronny Glover came to see me a little while ago."

"Oh?"

"I'm concerned, Penny." Oscar was more solemn than usual. She had planned to tell him about Ronny's two plagiarized paragraphs.

"What's up?" she asked. He was not laughing.

"He brought me this essay you had assigned and gave back to him. He says you gave him a C at first, even though you claimed two paragraphs were copied, but he says not. Then when he redid it and showed you in your office hour after class, you gave him an F because, you said then, the whole draft was plagiarized."

"Oh, yes. I didn't catch the first paragraph being copied until he fixed his typos." She laughed. "Ronny can't even plagiarize effectively."

Oscar wasn't smiling. "You should have caught it all the first time," he said. "He shouldn't have gotten that C."

"I made a mistake," Penny said. "I'm sorry."

Oscar got up and began pacing. "That's not good enough, Penny. Look, he can't write this well. He couldn't possibly write a sentence like this with a participle construction: 'Having done their lesson preparation for the next day, the students left the dorm and went to the gym to play basketball.' That construction is way beyond Ronny, the vocabulary, too. How could you miss it? It's so obvious."

He was extremely upset. He wasn't going to turn his rage on her, was he? He'd been so supportive. She was new, and this was her first mistake.

"You're smart. This is not hard to catch, Penny. We're letting these kids down, if we let them get away with this."

"I'm trying to stop it …" she started.

"You can't make mistakes like this," he went on, his voice louder. He hadn't heard her. "I bet I could give you a passage from this book," he said, pulling one out of his bookcase, "tell you to find the errors, and you wouldn't be able to."

She was thinking, I've been writing and publishing for years. I've taught essay writing for five years at the community college, but all she said was, "Okay." Let him test her editing skills, if that was what he wanted.

He put the book back. "These kids need us. We're their last hope. If they flunk out here, it's all over for them. This fucking place. It's a sinking ship, and all that's left on it are the rats." He had tears in his eyes.

We're not rats, the kids aren't rats, she was thinking, but he was pacing around, and she didn't think another apology would help, certainly not an argument. She waited.

"Penny, I've been catching this stuff for years. You can search their key word on the internet and find the essay." He handed her a computer print out. It was Ronny's essay on student extracurricular activities.

"Penny, I told you about that prison van I pass on my way to work. Ronny and Terence and many others are going to end up there if we don't help them."

Then she saw what lay beneath his anger. He had had to work so hard, stay so on top of his language, be so perfect to emerge from being a sharecropper's son, get his own HBCU degree, then his PhD in English from U.C.-Berkeley, and rise to be Associate Dean at the University of Illinois in Chicago that he had learned too cruelly that one false step and he'd fall down and never be able to get up again. But she, who'd had educated parents, been Valedictorian of her small high school class, a Phi Beta Kappa in college, could afford a few mistakes, could even laugh at them. She was white and had had all those privileges he had had to work so hard for. He couldn't laugh, but at least he'd stopped yelling. He was crying. She might get him to listen now.

"I'll do my very best, Oscar. I care about these kids, too. I need to go now. I have my office hours. I may have students waiting." Not to mention that she was so hungry, she felt faint.

"Wait a minute, Penny. I'm sorry I got so angry. It's not you. Everything's bad today."

She sat back down. If he wasn't worried about her office hours, she'd try not to be, but her feeling faint was another problem. She hoped she didn't pass out. Maybe if she didn't say much, he'd let her go sooner. She glanced at her watch. Only twenty minutes left in her office hours anyway. She did want to know what was bugging him that had made him turn on her. It was the last thing she'd expected.

"The new Provost," he said, standing in front of her, his eyes anxious. "Acting Provost, though not for long as acting, I'm afraid, is going to be that idiot Finance Officer, Robert Grubb, the one who's helping the President cook the books."

He began pacing again. "I can't believe the sheer gall of these so-called administrators. No integrity, no decency. It's criminal, is what it is. How can they expect the students to do well when they have no models for decent, honest behavior?"

Penny was relieved that he was attacking someone else. How could she hold his earlier rage against him? He was so passionate. He wanted so much for these young people, and his cause, his love of them, was so fraught with peril, so uphill, so nearly impossible of achievement. If it helped him to rage at her, let him. She would weather it and help him all she could. She'd learn how.

"Penny, this Grubb, I checked him out. He is a criminal. He served ten years for embezzlement in the 1980s, and they hired him here five years ago. I can't believe it. Stupid, absolutely stupid."

"They hired an embezzler? They thought he'd learned his lesson?"

"I doubt it." Oscar sat down at his desk, more relaxed now, and leaned forward toward her. "The former President, Angus Brown, ran this college into bankruptcy, probably with Grubb's help. Oh, no, I think they wanted his embezzling skills. What I can't figure out is where Audrey stood in all that. She was too close to the President not to have known what went on under Brown and what's going on now under Siler. I was pressing her about getting my budget. Hell, they don't give out budget information to any of the departments or divisions. We all work blind. The trustees are letting them get away with it. Did Audrey decide to call them on it and threaten to go to the trustees? She had some conscience, even if I couldn't always persuade her, and I know she got me hired. She knew the college wouldn't survive long unless they had better faculty and more students graduated. Their attrition rate is a disgrace. Only thirty percent of their entering freshmen graduate from here or any college."

"That bad?" Penny was surprised, even though she was learning firsthand how poorly prepared her students were even for the remedial courses.

Oscar was bitter. "They take these poor kids who have no chance of succeeding, run them through the mill here for a few years, collect their government scholarship and loan money, and then the kids either drop out or flunk out. I have students who are taking freshman comp for the fourth time. They let them hang on like that and keep raking in their money."

"That's sad," said Penny. She looked at her watch. No student would wait this long. It was ten to twelve. "I'd better go, Oscar. I need to eat. I'm feeling faint."

He jumped up. "Can I give you an apple? That's my lunch today."

"No, that's okay. I have my lunch with me. I just need to go eat it and see if any students came to my office hours." She stood up. The man did hang onto her.

"One more thing, Penny. I was going to tell you. Here's Grubb, the one I'd suspect if I suspected anyone at all. Arresting the husband was totally stupid. But you know who they hauled in to the police station in Riverdell this morning at eight o'clock?"

"Who?"

"Me. That idiot detective turned up at my house, scared my wife to death. I'd already left for campus. He came here, right to this office, and said he needed me to come in to answer some questions."

"Oh, no," said Penny, thinking of her conscientious friend Derek. He cared very much to solve this case, the sooner the better. He'd leave no stone unturned. Was he suspicious because Penny was reluctant to help him spy? Had Sammie told him something about Oscar's talking to her?

"Yes," he said grimly, holding her where she was with his eyes. "He wanted to know where I was Wednesday night, the night Audrey was killed. I told him I couldn't remember. I went for a long drive to sort out my thoughts, so I was out driving around about the time Audrey was killed."

Seven

Tuesday, February 20. When Penny ducked into the Writing Center just before noon in case any students were waiting, the room was empty except for a couple of young men using the computers, but they weren't her students. She was leaving for the library when Kenneth rounded the corner. He was wearing his navy blue and white guard uniform, though he didn't go on duty until three. He was smiling. "Hello, my love. Care for a spot of lunch?"

He was a relief, no doubt about that, after Oscar's passionate outbursts. Calm, steady Kenneth, who kept her sane. It was so easy to laugh with him about other people's absurdities, but she couldn't laugh with him about Oscar. That was hitting her below the belt. She needed Kenneth in his calm, happy mode, not jealous over her concern about Oscar. "I'd love lunch. I've been hungry since eleven, but I brought a sandwich."

"So did I, love, for my supper, but save yours. Let's try the staff dining room. My fellow guards are telling me the food's quite decent. A hot meal only costs four dollars."

"If what my students tell me is true, the cafeteria food is sickening. They're in the same building, right? Same kitchen? They say it's nasty."

He made a face. "Maybe it's a different set-up. Let's find out. Your students could be exaggerating." He rolled his eyes at her, then hugged her. "I'll take your books." He unhooked her backpack and slung it over his shoulder, and she followed him to the elevator.

Another mild, sunny day greeted them as they walked down the steps of Booher Hall. White and red tulips were opening next to the daffodils. "Lovely weather," said Kenneth. "We never have such days in February. If we did, the May blossom would be out. This is like late May on Gower."

"Some day I want to be on Gower when the hawthorn is blooming in the hedgerows," she said, "but a warm February is a delight and fairly common here. The peepers will be out along the Haw. We'll have to walk through the woods this weekend. Oh, and trout lilies may be out. I know a place where they bloom farther up the Haw from the dam."

They passed students lying on the grass in the sun. It was so warm that Penny shrugged out of her coat, with Kenneth helping, and carried it. "We could use some quiet time," he said. "We've had so much going on from the time our plane touched down."

They'd turned to walk down some steps to a lower plaza where the student union was located, including the cafeteria and bookshop. The building was one of the newer ones: square, concrete and brick. Kenneth pointed to a door at the corner nearest them. "I think that's where the staff eat." He held the door, and they entered a fairly small room set with eight tables, four chairs each, and a short serving line. On a separate, larger table were urns for coffee and hot water, tea bags, pitchers of ice water, iced tea, and various condiments.

"This table suit you, love?" Kenneth asked, and when she nodded, he set her backpack on one chair and draped her coat and his jacket over it. "Come meet Rosa, one of the other guards."

Rosa wore a large white apron and stood smiling behind a big tray of fried chicken. There was also a casserole of tuna and noodles. "Rosa, this is my wife, Penny."

Rosa gave Penny a genuine smile. "Pleased to meet you, Miss Penny. We all likes Mr. Kenneth. Will you have the chicken or the tuna casserole?"

"Chicken, please, and nice to meet you, too. The food looks great." She took mashed potatoes and gravy, fried okra, one of her favorites, and peach cobbler for dessert. While she unloaded her tray, Kenneth brought them each a cup of hot tea.

"You can deal with the tea bag tea?" asked Penny. At home they always used a good loose tea like Earl Grey or Darjeeling.

"Definitely. The water's hot, fortunately. Food doesn't look too nasty." He grinned at her.

"No. Hmm, not bad. Chicken's tasty, and I love fried okra. I wonder if the kids get the same food or different."

"I'll ask," he said.

"No, don't, but I bet they don't. Listen, I learned something from Oscar this morning. He said Derek took him in to question him. You know anything about that?"

"I knew he didn't trust the bloke, and I can't blame him. Your boss had a big row with the Provost, and then she was found dead."

Penny wanted to drop that conversation and start all over. They'd already been through this, but why was Derek picking on Oscar? She thought of several things she might say, but they'd probably all inflame her beloved.

She was sure Oscar wasn't guilty, but Kenneth would want to know what proof she had. Finally, she said what she'd started out to say. "Maybe Derek should talk to the guy who is taking the Provost's place, Rob Grubb."

"I haven't heard of him. Why would he want to talk to him?"

"According to Oscar, he served time in the 1980s for embezzlement, and Oscar thinks he and President Siler are cooking the books."

"That would be dumb, to embezzle again after you'd already served time. How long was he in for?"

"Ten years."

"And they hired him?"

"Yes, five years ago."

"That doesn't make him a murderer." Kenneth cut off a piece of chicken and looked thoughtfully at Penny. "What else did your chairman tell you?" He was totally serious and worried. She knew that frown.

"He told me he has no alibi for Wednesday night." Okay, he'd asked. So? Why shouldn't her boss tell her that? Why was Derek so suspicious of Oscar anyway?

"That's right, love. Your boss is looking quite like his primary suspect. Can't you see why, when he has no alibi?"

"He's no murderer," she found herself saying. "He's a good man, Kenneth. He cares about the kids. He wanted the Provost and the President to give them a chance to get their college degree. I don't think you see the man clearly."

"So he cares about the students. So you do, I know for a fact, but you don't scream at the Provost or manhandle young men out of your classroom."

"I lock the door at ten after," Penny said. "Kenneth, this is a difficult place to teach. You have to be tough with these kids. It's called tough love. Then, if you find out the higher-ups are screwing the kids, of course, you're angry. You might even yell."

He stared at her like she'd lost her mind.

"Penny, think. Someone killed the Provost, probably someone very angry at her, even if it was for good reasons. Good people sometimes do bad things."

Penny wished she hadn't said a word, had never mentioned Oscar Ferrell now. All she could see in her mind's eye was Oscar crying.

It was as they were walking back up the steps to the main part of the campus that they ran into Merilee and Ronny. He had one of his huge arms around her shoulders. Merilee saw them first and stopped. "Hey, Miz Weaver." She glanced at Kenneth and then back to Penny. Ronny was studying the sidewalk.

"Hello, Merilee and Ronny. I believe you've both met my husband, Mr. Morgan. He's a security guard here now."

"Yes, sir," said Ronny, looking at Kenneth briefly but still avoiding Penny's eyes.

"Are you two off to study?" Penny asked.

"No, ma'am. We're going to check our boxes. My mama writes me every week."

"I'd like to talk to your mama, Merilee. Can you give me her phone number?"

"Yes, ma'am." Penny retrieved her backpack from Kenneth and found a pen and a scrap of paper. She noted the number down. "Thanks, Merilee. Ronny, I talked with Dr. Ferrell about your paper. Remember, I gave you several possible topics. I think you'd better choose one of those and start your essay all over. I'm sure you have lots to say about Camden, or maybe whether it's better to be single or married." She smiled, but Ronny kept staring at the ground. It was Merilee who said to Penny, "Yes, ma'am. I have to write two more paragraphs, too. C'mon, Ronny. 'Bye, Miz Weaver, 'bye, Mr. Morgan."

The young couple walked on past them although Ronny hadn't said another word. Kenneth turned and watched them walk down the steps toward the student union.

"He's the one pumping himself full of steroids, right?"

"Right," she said. "You heard Obie say that the coach won't do anything about it."

They walked on. "How does Ronny do in your class?"

"He copied an essay from the internet. That's why he has to start over. I gave him an F."

"He was pretty unfriendly. Did he complain to your boss?"

"Yes."

"Penny, he's in bad shape, physically and probably mentally."

"She's in worse shape mentally," Penny said. She'd vowed to herself she wouldn't bring up the subject of Oscar, but she said, "She's learning disabled, and Oscar thinks she's retarded, too." Thankfully, he didn't bristle at the name of her boss. He was focused on Merilee.

"And she's in college?"

"Yes, and she can't write legibly or spell. Oh, Kenneth, it's so sad. Sammie has seen her test scores. She can barely read. She's one of the few students who has a book, but I doubt she can read it. That's why I want to talk to her mother."

Kenneth put his arm around her shoulders. Was he feeling protective or maybe wanting to close the distance they'd both felt after their lunch discussion? She hated it when they fought. It didn't happen often, but since she'd taken this job, it was happening every few days. Not good. She was determined to do her best at this job for Oscar's sake and for the kids, who were already getting to her even though she felt like knocking their heads together sometimes. She and Kenneth had always talked freely about their work and interests, but probably she'd better keep her new, confusing feelings about Oscar to herself.

"Merilee might as well throw herself in the rubbish bin if she takes up with Ronny," he said and squeezed her shoulders.

"I know," she said.

~

Penny stared at the poster of Zora Neale Hurston that always drew her to that third floor corner of the library. It was from the front cover of an anthology of Hurston's work, *I Love Myself When I Am Laughing, and Then Again When I Am Looking Mean and Impressive*. Zora wore a coat with a mink collar, gloves, and a hat closely fitted to her head, with a feather across the front. Her face was alive with amusement. Her eyes were half-shut, her mouth open to show her white, even teeth, and her broad nose over a wide smile seemed part of just how much delight she took in life, in everything.

I need your help, Zora, she was thinking as she turned over the last of the autobiographies she'd been reading. These students need you, your indomitable spirit, your laughter, your ability to be mean and impressive, and all they have is me. I'll do my best.

"Hi, girlfriend, can I bother you?" Sammie.

Penny glanced at her watch. Two-thirty. "Of course. Have a seat. I could use a break. What's new?"

Today Sammie was wearing a russet brown skirt and vest with a pale yellow silk blouse. Her hair was pulled into an elegant twist over her left ear, which Penny suspected was a wig. She'd tried to figure that out on the drive in that morning and failed. She herself felt wilted, her long-sleeved red pullover too warm for this February day, and the library heating was on, though she liked this corner partly, too, because it was the coolest. The library on the third floor was always too hot, but Sammie looked as fresh and crisp as she'd looked that morning.

"I'm furious at Derek."

"Why?"

"He arrested Oscar, the dumb shit."

"Arrested? But he's out, he's here. Derek told you?"

"No, Oscar told me. He had to post bail, and he can't leave town. We met today to work on the interdisciplinary seminar. I want so bad to do women's studies, lit and history. Here I am, all excited about finally getting to do it. Then Oscar tells me my husband arrested him this morning so he's not as prepared as he'd hoped to be for our meeting. Talk about being embarrassed."

"He told me about being taken in," Penny said. "I don't get it either. Oscar rages, for sure. He raged at me today, but ..."

"He did? I thought he was so happy with you. The word is he thinks he pulled a real coup, hiring a published writer to teach our students to write. Whoever would have thought that college freshmen could learn to write from an actual writer?" She grinned at Penny, who suddenly felt the morning's and the noontime's burdens roll off her.

"So what did you do to set off our dear supportive Oscar? It must have been really bad, Penny."

Suddenly Penny was laughing. It was all so terrible but funny, too. "I didn't catch Ronny's plagiarism fast enough. I caught some of it and told him to redo it, but the next time he showed it to me, he'd fixed all his typos, and I could see it was completely someone else's. So I gave him an F, and he ran straight to Oscar."

"Oh, girl, that is too funny. So he screamed at you? He must be losing it."

Penny was laughing so hard she found it hard to continue. "He didn't scream, but he ranted and raved awhile. He insisted I should know better. We had to be smarter than these kids. But then he started crying. He wants so much to help these kids. I do, too, Sammie. Then he handed me Ronny's essay straight off the internet."

"It'll drive you nuts, these kids, terrible and wonderful all at once." Sammie had tears in her eyes. "Damn, this is hard stuff, but he don't need to be yelling at you, Penny. You're on his side. I heard he yelled at Clarkson the other day. Wish I could've heard that."

"Yes, I heard him."

"You heard him and didn't tell me?"

"So much has been going on, I forgot. But Clarkson and President Siler seemed very thick on the elevator immediately afterwards. Clarkson has tenure, she reminded him, and Oscar doesn't even have a contract."

"My God, this college is the pits. What are they thinking of? They'll go right down the tubes. Oscar is like gold to them, and they're treating him like shit."

"I know. I think that, plus the arrest, plus Grubb being made Acting Provost is all getting him down. Ronny's silly essay must have put him over the top."

"So Grubb's got the Provost slot? At least Clarkson doesn't. I was so afraid."

"Grubb is bad, too," said Penny. She so needed to talk to somebody. "You won't tell Derek all this? He wants me to spy."

"Me, too. I told him, find your own darned suspects. I'm at this college to teach students, not spy on the faculty. Wait till I get home. He's gonna hear my opinion on his dragging Oscar off to the police station."

Penny smiled. "Poor Derek. He never does well when we gang up on him."

"You better believe it, but I'm telling him who to arrest."

"Grubb?"

"No, Clarkson. The bastard had been having an affair with the Provost before she got killed. For over a year, I heard. She probably wouldn't put out, and he killed her." Sammie laughed.

~

Penny was cutting up vegetables for a pot of borscht later Tuesday afternoon when Sarah knocked and opened the door, Seb on one hip. "Ga-ma." Seb held out his arms to her, and Penny put down her big chopping knife and picked him up.

"Hi, Sarah. What's up?"

Seb wriggled to get down. Penny walked over and shut the bathroom door, pulled a cardboard box of toys off the bottom shelf of the bookcase and put it in the middle of the living room for Seb.

"I need you to keep Seb for me, Mom."

"Now?"

"Yes, if you don't mind."

Penny thought of her plan to prepare her lessons for Thursday and also get the borscht going. Kenneth wouldn't be home until eleven-thirty, so she'd thought of working on a new poem once her course work was caught up. Sarah was frowning, and this was the first time she'd seen her for several days. Was she still angry? "You don't have anybody else to keep him?" Penny went back to dicing cabbage.

"No, Mom. That's why I'm asking you." She was definitely still angry.

"You asked Leroy?" She knew he was home. He'd driven his work van in half an hour earlier.

"I need to talk to Leroy, Mom. Without Seb. So will you?"

Penny hoped Sarah wasn't going to cut Leroy off now. It wasn't a good time in her life to do as much babysitting as Leroy was so eager to do, and Leroy's anguish she couldn't begin to imagine.

She used her knife to ease the chopped cabbage into the soup pot. "How long do you need me for?"

"About two hours, I think. I hope. Mom, Leroy has decided he wants to marry me. We have to talk. Tonight's the best time. He's free, I'm free. So can you?"

Sarah wasn't stamping her foot in impatience, but she might as well have been.

"I will," said Penny. "It's nearly five now. Can you get Seb by eight at the latest? Then I can still get some work done tonight."

"Mom, he'll be asleep by eight, but I should be back before eight. Here's his diaper bag. He can eat whatever you're having for supper." She turned to go.

"Borscht."

"What, Mom?"

"I'm having borscht, Russian beet soup, and bread."

"He'll eat anything, Mom. He's two now. He has a full set of teeth. She put her hand on the door, then turned. "Thanks, Mom," a little less angry, then, "'Bye, Seb. Mama be back soon. 'Bye 'bye."

Seb waved his arms, opening and closing his fist, and Sarah was out the back door. He went back to exploring the old salt boxes and cocoa tins that Penny saved for visiting children. She pulled out a sauce pan, a couple of wooden spoons, a set of plastic measuring spoons looped together, and gave those to him, too. If she could get the potatoes peeled and into the soup, she'd give him her full attention. They should be able to eat by six. So Leroy had gotten wind of Sarah's new boyfriend and wanted to marry her at the same time that Sarah was planning to drop Leroy from her life. It all made her feel helpless, and this baby was caught in the middle.

She had just dropped the last potato in and turned the heat up under her big Dutch oven when Leroy's rooster crowed. This was Formaldehyde IV. Leroy had begun his first flock in 1993, and he killed all the older chickens every three years and started a new flock of a dozen hens and one rooster, always named Formy, in memory of their success in getting the local Sampson Pine plant to stop polluting huge amounts of formaldehyde. Formy, like a watch dog, often announced visitors.

Penny looked out the door at the top of the stairs and turned on their porch light. Derek was ascending, clipboard in hand. When he'd called over the weekend, she'd said she hadn't learned that much, to talk to Kenneth, who was getting to know some of the students. But now maybe she'd try to direct him toward Clarkson and Grubb and away from Oscar, though she would have to be careful how she did that. Sammie was hoping to do the same thing. She didn't know how Sammie would approach it, but she herself would try not to make it a barrage. Slip in the idea without fanfare.

She opened the door to him before he knocked. "Come on in, Derek. Would you like some tea or coffee?"

"Thanks, Penny. Coffee, if it's easy."

"There's some left from breakfast, in the refrigerator. That all right?"

"That would be great. Why, hello there, young man."

Seb had left his pans and spoons and come over to investigate the visitor.

"I think you've met Seb, Derek, Sarah's baby. Seb, this is my friend, Mr. Derek. Sit anywhere, Derek. I'll just stick this in the microwave."

Seb was pointing to Derek's baseball cap, which he'd set on his clipboard. It had "Shagbark County Sheriff" printed on the front. Seb patted his head and reached for the cap.

Derek caught on and put the cap on Seb's head backwards. Seb reached up and pulled it off, then tried to put it back on. The cap fell on the floor, and Derek picked it up and put it on Seb again.

"What can I do for you, Derek?" Penny asked as she handed him his cup and sat down opposite him with a cup of her own. Seb was occupied with the hat for now, and the vegetables needed to simmer awhile before she added the cooked beets and chicken.

Derek picked up his clipboard. "You can give me anything you've learned at the college. Kenneth keeps me posted on what he's learning, but tell me anything you've observed since you went to work there, a week ago today, right?"

"Right. Hard to believe it has only been a week. So much has happened."

"What, for instance?" Derek asked casually. He was trying to be polite, not pushy, but she knew he was there to push.

Penny got up and turned down the soup. It was easy enough to tell him to lay off Oscar and consider Grubb and Clarkson, but how to convince him? Conniving wasn't her usual mode, but before she had told him "not much." Maybe she would continue that theme and let him draw it out of her, as if she were reluctant, not eager to tell him, so he would discover it for himself. A good teacher was supposed to do that, set up the learning so that the students were discovering. He did trust her. Plus, she did honestly believe that Grubb and Clarkson were much more likely suspects, though almost anybody was more likely than Oscar.

"I don't know many people outside the English Department, and not even many of those in my department yet. I'm getting to know my students, and there's Sammie, of course. She hears more gossip than I do. Have you talked to her?"

"Yes, Penny." He was making an effort to be patient. She could hear it in his voice. "I do talk to Sammie. It's you I want to hear from now. We've worked together before, Penny. Remember your famous intuition? I want you to use it. Help me here, Penny. This is a big case, and I've got very little to go on."

"You took Oscar in," she said. "He was pretty offended." She watched Seb stirring her wooden spoon around inside the cap and then putting the cap on his head.

"I know that, Penny. He is a suspect but not the only one. I've got several leads, but I'm missing too much. Do you know what Audrey White was like, for instance? I can't figure out why anyone would want to kill her."

"I only met her once, Derek. An attractive woman, second in command at the college, very close to the President, apparently. Not a boat rocker. Neither she nor the President is readily available to the faculty or the students. They hide in their offices. I saw the President for the first time only last Thursday and by chance as I was leaving the building."

"Tell me about that." Derek was grasping at straws and trying very hard to be patient with her.

Seb ran over to Derek suddenly with the cap and pointed to Derek's head. "Hat," he said.

Derek took it and put it on his head.

Seb reached for it, and Derek put it on Seb's head. "Hat," said Seb and went back to his spoon and salt boxes.

"She and Clarkson got on the elevator when I did. I didn't know who she was at first. I'd met him, but I figured out from their conversation that she was Christine Siler. He seemed very respectful of her power and maybe worried, because I'm sure the word is out among the students that he gave Merilee an A in exchange for sex."

"Sammie told me all about that," he said as if it didn't interest him or didn't seem relevant. She could have predicted that he didn't want to listen to Sammie.

"These are just my impressions. Clarkson is apparently one of the few faculty with tenure, which she was reminding him. He could, however, be fired for sexual misconduct, but she seemed to be reassuring him that he wouldn't be. He's under her thumb though. He treated her like a very big cheese."

"She is," said Derek, "President of the college."

"Then did you know that the new Provost is going to be the Vice President for Financial Affairs? All the money decisions, at least keeping track of income and expenditures, goes through his office now, and he's unavailable most of the time, too, I understand. So he has moved up to second in command, in charge of academic as well as financial affairs. Then I guess you knew that he served time for embezzlement?"

"No, I didn't. What's his name?"

"Grubb. Robert Grubb. The last President, Angus Brown, who hired him five years ago, ran the college into bankruptcy. Christine Siler was hired, Malvina says, to pull it out of debt and also keep it accredited. I'm teaching

Pre-Composition to kids, some of whom only read at grade school level, but they used to throw all the freshmen into regular Freshman Composition, and they mostly failed. The school only kept its accreditation because they set up remedial courses. So these kids they accept can get into St. Francis even if no other school will take them and have a better chance of getting a college degree, but most lack the skills or the habits of study and discipline. To me that's so sad."

Derek bristled. "At least these students they take in have their opportunity. If they throw it away, that's sad. It's not sad that the college takes them. My high school grades were terrible, Penny. I joined the Army and gradually got my skills up and my grades so I could get into college, but nobody helped me. Those kids are luckier than they know. Then to have good teachers like you and Sammie who want to help them?"

He set his clipboard on the couch. "If there's nothing else, I'd better get going."

Penny didn't think she could say anything more that would convince him that something was terribly wrong at St. Francis. He was listening, but he wasn't hearing her. She wanted to argue with Derek that the students weren't able to use their opportunity; but as she stood to say goodbye, all she could see in her mind's eye was the prison van. She had also seen that prison van when she and Sammie drove past the local prison. If Derek couldn't see it, then she didn't think she could make him see it.

Sarah had not returned by eight, so Penny had opened their fold-out bed and tucked Seb into it after reading him *Good Night, Moon* until his eyes closed. Then she worked at the kitchen table with the main apartment lights off and only the kitchen lamp on. She caught up on her college work but didn't get to a poem, and there was no word from Sarah, who hadn't returned by ten-thirty. Penny was exhausted and lay down near Seb to nap until either Sarah or Kenneth returned.

She had a strange and vivid dream just before someone knocked at the door. She was carrying Seb and trying to find Kenneth. She was in a big crowd of people like that at a state fair and had neither money nor food. She had lost her wallet as well as their lunch. Seb began crying, and she had to find food for him and for herself. She was so hungry. If only she could find Kenneth. She didn't see anyone she knew. Then finally she saw Ronny. He seemed to be part of an act, a big muscle man lifting bar bells. She asked him for help, but he told her to clear off. Only paying customers. He yelled, "Get out of my life," as she walked away. Then she saw Kenneth way across a huge milling crowd of people, but though she called to him, he didn't hear her and got farther and farther away.

For a minute after she woke up, she didn't realize someone was at the door. Just as she had roused, Seb had begun crying. "It's okay, Seb. It's just somebody knocking." She picked him up and lurched toward the door, steadying herself as she passed the kitchen table.

Sarah entered, looking embarrassed. "I'm so sorry, Mom." She took Seb into her arms as he leaned toward her. "Sebbie, you've been sleeping?"

"Yes, he went to sleep at eight, like you said. Sarah, I need you to come back for him at a reliable time."

"I'm sorry, Mom. I couldn't help it. It was really hard to tell Leroy that I don't want to marry him and probably I'll marry Brian some day. We're going to live together, starting in March. I'm moving out of my apartment and in with Brian. Gee, it's only a week."

Penny sat down. She saw that it was eleven-thirty, and Kenneth would be home any minute. She was so groggy. Not a good time to talk.

Besides, she was too angry at Sarah for making her blithe assumptions about other people's feelings—little Seb's, Leroy's, hers. Sarah was twenty-eight. Penny kept thinking she'd mature faster than she actually did. Sarah certainly had a penchant for leaving people hanging. Penny was afraid to ask if she had told Leroy he couldn't see Seb any more. So she nodded. Arguments could wait. Sarah and Seb needed to get home.

"I told Leroy that I wouldn't need him to babysit as much, that Brian would help me."

Penny closed her eyes. In many ways, Seb was all Leroy had. She and Kenneth, Andy and Jan, and Belle and Kate were all good friends and a kind of family for him, but Seb was everything to him. "I'm sorry about that, Sarah. Leroy loves him so much."

"I know, Mom. I told you it was hard. We talked a long time. He wanted to make love for the last time, and I said okay. Maybe I did the wrong thing. Why is this so hard?"

Penny thought, you're making it hard, but she didn't say it.

Then she heard Kenneth's key in the lock. Finally.

"Hi, love," Kenneth said to Sarah as he hugged her and Seb. "And my lovely wife is awake. Super. Sarah, want to join us for a milky drink? Seb looks ready for a party."

As indeed did the baby, reaching out his arms to Kenneth, who took him and lay down on the floor, putting Seb on his stomach. Seb was delighted.

Penny moved to the stove to warm some milk. "You'll stay a minute, Sarah?"

Sarah nodded and sat down on the edge of the fold-up bed.

"Cocoa or Ovaltine?"

"Cocoa. Do you have any marshmallows?"

"Coming up." Penny was always amazed at how Kenneth could help her pull back from being really grouchy or too serious when a situation needed a lighter touch. He must have sensed the tension when he came in. He defused it so quickly.

The baby squealed with delight as Kenneth rolled him over and tickled him. Penny wished she could enjoy her grandson without worrying so much about him.

Kenneth got up on hands and knees and growled at Seb, who ran happily screaming to his mother. Then he ran back at Kenneth, shrieking, "Go 'way."

But Kenneth growled again to Seb's shriek of delight. Monster was a game they both loved.

When the cocoa was ready, they moved to the kitchen table, and Kenneth held Seb's cup of milk for him and said to Sarah, "You must enjoy him so much. I hate to miss being around him, watching him grow and change when we're off in Wales. He remembers the monster game, amazingly. Smart lad. You must be proud."

Sarah nodded, tears running down her face. "I am," she said, her voice catching, "but it's hard sometimes, you know? To raise him alone, and I want a family for him."

"We're family, Sarah," Kenneth said quietly. He broke a digestive biscuit and gave half to Seb.

"I know," said Sarah, "but you're so far away when you're in Wales. I get so lonely sometimes."

Ah, thought Penny, there's the crux. She put her arms around Sarah, relieved that she had let them see what was underneath all these harsh decisions she'd been making. Penny remembered how lonely she had felt when she'd finally said "enough is enough" to her marriage to Sarah's father. Of course, it was hard to be a single parent. She'd had three children. Sarah was younger, and of course she wanted a better life for herself, all understandable. But would Brian give it to her, and how would Seb and Leroy cope with losing each other?

Eight

Thursday, February 22. "I can't announce in the middle of a Black History Convocation that the college is corrupt and should fire its President, Oscar, much as I'd love to." Rick Clegg was in a good mood this Thursday morning an hour before he was due to speak at the convocation being held at eleven in the gym. He smiled at his old friend and then at Penny.

"I don't see why not," said Oscar, taking his feet off his desk and sitting up in his chair. "You know how bad it is. Siler is ruining this place, if there was anything left to ruin after Angus Brown got done doing his damage. He fired all the qualified faculty and kept all the duds that kissed his ass. You know that's true."

Rick stretched his legs. He was dressed carefully in an impeccably tailored grey suit with the jacket unbuttoned, giving pride of place to a tie with starbursts of color looking like Fourth of July firecrackers in red, blue, yellow, orange and violet. His black shoes were new and highly polished, and he wore gold cuff links. "Oscar, I told you this college would try your patience and test your mettle. You're a catalyst, like Penny here." He put his arm around her. "The two of you are God's gift to this struggling institution. Some would say we no longer need black colleges now that the majority of colleges have opened their doors to us, but we know that to hold onto our cultural heritage and identity ..." He leaned forward and looked intently at Oscar. "… we need not only our churches, our music, our literature, our art, but also our colleges.

"Penny sees the point, and so do you. You're angry because a few fools are getting away with murder." He turned suddenly to Penny. "Interesting slip. Maybe there is a connection between the corruption that's driving Oscar nuts and the death of Audrey White? Heaven help us, if so. But, Oscar, look at the students you do have. They need you, Penny, Sammie, Obie, and all the other good people employed here. Yes, there are problems at the top, but even you, Oscar, don't know exactly what they are or who's running the show."

"Siler, obviously, Rick," said Oscar, slamming his fist on his desk.

"How do you know it's not higher, the trustees? Or lower, Grubb or even Clarkson? You know what, Oscar? In my experience, behind every corrupt black person, some white person is either benefitting or colluding. Half the trustees are white. Why aren't they doing their job? Why don't they demand a financial accounting? Why don't they lay down the law about admission standards or insist that these ill-qualified students be given the extra help they require? Why don't they get tough on drugs?"

"Rick, I'd go to them in a minute if I thought it would do any good, but Siler has them all in her pocket. They'll be there today, by the way, and all the major faculty. Adjuncts like Penny have been asked to go and to let their classes out, but the full-time faculty members are required to go, and all their students. Here's your opportunity to give them some truth, damn it."

Rick smiled, first at Penny, who knew how committed Rick was to truth-telling, then at Oscar. "Oh, I'll be talking about truth, Oscar, my old friend. When have I not? But hopefully it will slide in like a stiletto, straight to the heart."

Oscar's phone rang. Penny glanced at her watch. Nearly ten-thirty. They had only half an hour to get over to the gym. She and Sammie were leaving at ten-forty from Sammie's office, but Rick and Oscar probably should leave soon. It was a ten-minute walk.

Oscar handed the phone to Penny, who stood up. "Yes? I'm Ms. Weaver. Thanks for getting back to me, Mrs. Taylor. Yes, I'm concerned about Merilee. I have her in the first English Composition course. She did turn in her homework, and it was correct. The problem is that she reads very poorly and writes like a much younger child. Yes, I'm aware that she had special education classes all the way through school and received her high school diploma, but she's not ready for college, Mrs. Taylor. She is unable to read her textbook or do her assignments in class. Then she brings me homework with perfect answers. I don't believe that she's doing her own work outside of class. You've been helping her? I can understand that you want to help her, Mrs. Taylor, but to pass my course, she'll need to take tests and do work in class that she has to do by herself.

"Yes, I told her that she could type things, but she'll need to write in class, too. Could you tell me the kind of learning disability she has? Maybe the college can get her a tutor if we know." Penny listened, unbelieving.

"No, I'm afraid she can't drop this course. This isn't even a course for credit. She has to pass this one to be able to take the regular Freshman Composition course, and she needs two of those courses to graduate."

Penny handed Oscar the phone. "She hung up on me, Oscar. Her mother says Merilee had a very high fever shortly after she was born and suffered brain damage."

~

Penny and Sammie had found seats near the front on the left of the gym, behind Sheila, Lashandra and Letitia. The young women turned and smiled at them. The gym must have had five or six hundred folding chairs set out. The student body was over five hundred. It was still a gym, but a podium had been set up, and potted plants, with some lilies in vases, were arranged around the podium in the front. Penny noted faculty gathering in the back on the right. "Are you supposed to be sitting with the regular faculty, Sammie?"

Sammie put her arm around Penny's shoulder. She was dressed today in shades of purple, including mauve, fuchsia, violet and lilac. Penny couldn't name them all. Her blouse was a riot of purples, the print of irises and violets of all shades. Her suit skirt and jacket were a quieter mauve, and she wore deep purple earrings shaped like violets. "I belong here," she said, "with the students and you. Besides, we've got good seats for watching the whole show, and it will be a show. Look, there's Christine. The girls in front heard her, too, and they all watched as President Siler, in a sober black suit and heels, walked down the center aisle, followed by a stout man with brown curly hair and light skin with freckles. "That's Grubb," Sammie said, "right behind her." He also wore a black suit, complete with vest. His suit jacket was buttoned over his beer belly and straining at its seams.

"Interesting," said Penny. Slightly behind them walked Rick and then Clarkson, also in a black suit. No wrinkled suit jacket with leather elbow patches today.

"What's she got Clarkson doing," whispered Sammie, "the prayer?" Penny wanted to laugh but contained herself. The four bigwigs sat down in the front row on the right side, and then the faculty began to file in and take seats on the right behind them. Most of them wore black or grey as tribute to their dead Provost, Penny assumed. After they were seated, students who were still arriving were allowed to find seats. Penny looked for Oscar but didn't see him. Finally, she saw him slip in behind a group of students and find a seat in the back row.

After everyone had settled, the President rose and went to the mike at the podium. "Good morning, ladies and gentlemen."

"Good morning," echoed the audience.

"Please rise. After our invocation by Professor Clarkson we'll begin by singing 'Lift Every Voice and Sing.' We want to dedicate this convocation to our dear Provost, Dr. Audrey White, whom we lost so tragically last week."

They all stood, and Penny, even knowing all she did about the college's problems, felt moved by all the voices, young and old, mostly black, but some white, singing the song also called the "Negro National Anthem." It ached of suffering and sorrow sustained and survived, its rolling rhythms testament to a people's endurance and a triumph not yet arrived but even now wholeheartedly believed in.

Siler motioned the crowd to be seated and asked the chorus to join her in front. Forty or so students, wearing white blouses and black pants or skirts, moved into position, forming two rows in front of the audience, and began singing a medley of spirituals, beginning with "Nobody Knows de Trouble I've Seen" and ending with "He's Got the Whole World in His Hands," the solo sung, to Penny's astonishment, by Merilee. Her alto voice was strong and sure. When she sang, she was no longer the shy girl whom Penny had hardly been able to hear, but a proud, confident young woman singing words she obviously believed to be true. When she sang, "He's got the itty bitty baby in his hands," Penny thought of Seb. She hoped Seb was in good hands.

After Clarkson had read a list of men and women who had founded and contributed both to the college and to the "African American journey to freedom, equality, and dignity," as he put it, Christine Siler asked Robert Grubb to introduce "our speaker, the Reverend Richard Clegg."

Penny was curious about what Grubb would say. From all she knew of Grubb, none of it flattering, it seemed a shame that he was introducing Rick. She remembered Rick's words about telling the truth and wondered how he'd carry that off. She loved hearing Rick speak and always felt better afterwards.

Grubb called him "Brother Rick" and listed his achievements, his BA from Berkeley, his Bachelor of Divinity and PhD in Nuclear Science from Duke University. He reminded the audience that Brother Rick was serving as Commissioner for Shagbark County and had all his life worked for justice and the betterment of his people, with a focus on environmental health. Rob welcomed him to the mike with a handshake and left Brother Rick to tell the audience what he would.

Sammie grabbed Penny's hand and squeezed it. "This'll be good," she said.

Penny smiled and squeezed hers back. "Of course."

Rick let the crowd settle. Penny knew he'd wait until he had their full attention. He was solemn, but as he looked out at the faces turned to him, Penny sensed how much he cared for this college, its students, faculty, even its administrators, however poorly they did their jobs, however weak they were in a moral crisis.

"It's an honor to be here, my friends," he began. "For you all are my friends, or should we say, my brothers and sisters. I know some of you here better than others, but I know, like that song of ours says, that we are indeed all held in His hands. Not only the itty bitty baby, but the gambling man, the drug salesman, the alcoholic, those who abuse their power and those who suffer that abuse, those who love their work and their students or their teachers, those who are here only to collect their salary or their scholarship money. For we are all, rich, poor, old, young, black, white, powerful, powerless, experienced or new to everything in college life--we are all in His hands. Everything we do is known.

"When we act, when we speak, we leave traces of ourselves, and I'm not talking about DNA. Our spirits imprint themselves on those around us. Oh, yes, we leave our mark. No evil we do will not be known by Him, and eventually by others, but so also will our good leave its passage behind us. Others seeing what we have tried to do will be inspired to try harder themselves. We are held in His hand. We are loved. We are lovable, even in our errors, our weaknesses, our stumbling and falling on our faces. Oh, yes, we are loved. We will always pick ourselves up and keep going, because we are human. It takes a lot to stop us once we commit ourselves and make up our minds about something. We are all human, and we all have the ability and the challenge to be the best human beings we can be. But African Americans, because of their history in this country, have a special challenge in this, the new millennium, to come to a new understanding of the freedom we have sought for so long and so persistently."

All Penny could think of was that he was doing it. He was speaking the truth, and those guilty--and in the way he told it, they were all guilty–couldn't avoid their guilt. She thought of Oscar, who was so upset by the mischief being done at the top. Even Oscar was guilty of not believing enough in his power to bring about change. Rick's greatness of spirit was so refreshing. She felt lifted up and out of all her worries. She let out a sigh and focused on what he was saying again.

"Today I want us to think about the word *freedom* that has so beguiled Americans but especially African Americans, who arrived as slaves and were, in the beginning, not free at all. Historically, we have slowly but surely won many freedoms, which we may call our civil liberties. We have the freedom to be our own masters, not slaves to another master. We have the freedom to learn to read and write, which, you remember, most slaves did not have. We have the freedom to change our place of residence or business. We may now keep the money we earn, and we have the freedom to spend it as we choose. We have the freedom to bear and bring up our own children. No master will seed us with his seed or sell our babies away from us. We have all the freedom and all the responsibility, not only to keep and cherish our children but to help them grow into mature, caring adults. We have the freedom to go to college, to seek any profession we choose, to marry whom we will, to travel, to invest money, to choose our friends and buy homes and cars and other things we need, but most of all we have the one freedom without which all the other freedoms are meaningless. We have the freedom to be ourselves, to speak in our own voice and give voice to the truth as we see it. People may not like our truth or want to hear it. People may be cruel to us when we speak truth. They may deny that our truth is the truth. They may even kill us for speaking what we know to be true. But no one can kill the truth because the truth will out. Beautiful or ugly, yes, truth will always come out, no matter how much we stop our ears or shout for the truth teller to be silent, to go away.

"The truth will out because we are held in His hand, and so held, we all know in our hearts what is true. We can fool others and ourselves, but we can't fool that inside part of us that recognizes truth when it hears it. I leave you with this thought. Be truthful in your words and deeds. That is the true meaning of freedom. For the truth will set you free."

~

Café Green, near the N.C. State University campus on Hillsborough Street, was still crowded when they arrived a little after one o'clock following the convocation. Oscar had reserved a room in the back and invited her and Kenneth, Sammie and Derek, as well as Rick and Cathy, to have lunch there. Cathy had another commitment and couldn't make it, but Oscar's wife, Maudy, was waiting with Oscar when they got there.

Café Green was well known locally. The restaurant grew its produce, the meat and eggs it served, on the farm it also owned in rural Wake County. The meat and chicken came from animals that had not been treated with hormones or antibiotics. The vegetables and fruit were grown without pesticides or chemical fertilizers. They had an excellent chef. Penny hadn't eaten there often, but it made a nice change from her usual peanut butter and honey sandwich and raw carrots. She and Kenneth had brought Rick, and she told him during the short drive how she thought he had achieved his goal, getting to the heart of the matter at the college but in such a way that no one would have any excuse to get his or her hackles up. "Brilliant, Rick," she said, "and inspiring. I've been feeling weighed down by problems like Merilee's inability to do the work and the drugs that are everywhere here."

"There will always be drugs," Rick said, "of one kind or another. TV can be a drug, sex can be a drug, but you, Oscar, Sammie, Obie can give them other options, better choices. Drugs can appeal when they're the only game in town. Remember that there are other games, and you four have knowledge about those other ways of living one's life. You'd be surprised how susceptible these young people can be to adults who care and can imagine them succeeding in ways they haven't themselves yet imagined.

"Do you know that story of the three young black men from the inner city of Philadelphia, who vowed to be doctors and made a pact with each other and supported each other all the way through college and medical school?

They're doing their residencies now. Tell your students stories like that. You know how, Penny."

His words were apparently reassuring to Kenneth, who added, "I've already seen how quickly they drop all that tough talk when you can get them onto serious topics. I think I might be of help, too."

"Of course," said Rick and Penny together.

Oscar and Maudy led them back to the reserved dining room, and they were settled at the round table set for seven when Derek and Sammie arrived. Penny wondered how Derek would take this luncheon with one of his suspects. She was surprised both that Oscar had invited him and that Derek had come. Sammie must have had something to do with it. It would give Kenneth a chance to know Oscar better, too, and maybe he wouldn't be so suspicious and/or jealous, if that's what it was. Of course, she had some work to do on her feelings, too.

Oscar stood up to welcome Derek and Sammie. Rick's talk seemed to have buoyed him up, as well. He turned happy eyes on Penny and told Kenneth he was so delighted that he could join them, too. Kenneth was his usual friendly self, which disarmed most people he was meeting for the first time. To Penny's relief he was entirely cordial to Oscar.

Maudy helped, too. She was petite, not much more than five feet, so light-skinned that she could pass for white, and her hair was light brown and naturally straight. She was impeccably dressed in a light green suit with a blouse in subtle greens and blues. She smiled often, showing an attractive dimple, but didn't say a lot. She did tell Penny and Kenneth that she was so happy to meet them. She knew that Oscar had felt very lucky to get someone as qualified as Penny at the last minute. She hadn't known that Kenneth was also working at the college, but she was delighted to learn that and hoped he liked the job. A very important one, she emphasized, especially now with the Provost having been killed.

Rick was an old friend, and she hugged him and inquired about Cathy and his sons. Penny had felt some tension in the room when Derek and Sammie first entered. Derek's eyes sought Penny's, and he shook his head as though doubtful that he should be there. Sammie, however, walked right over to Maudy and led her to meet Derek. Oscar looked lost after he'd said his welcome speech. Penny knew he hadn't thought much of Derek from their early encounters. Oscar also watched Derek seek out Rick, who was his pastor. Derek and Sammie were both Deacons in the Ebenezer Baptist Church. Penny thought how Oscar was outnumbered in several senses.

Finally, Rick got Derek over to talk to Oscar. Penny heard Derek say, "Thank you for having Sammie and me along today. Rick's our treasured friend, and yours, too, I understand. I could use your advice. I'm going to need to talk to some students, and I'm not sure the best way to proceed." Penny and Kenneth, without making a conscious decision, both moved closer to Derek and Oscar. Sammie was still chatting with Maudy.

"We're still following leads." Derek didn't look at Oscar. "But it's possible a student killed her, given some of the evidence we now have. I realize the college will be resistant to our talking to students. We can do it quietly, but how would you suggest we approach it?"

That finally broke the ice among them.

They all settled to the table again, Penny on Oscar's right and Sammie on his left. Kenneth was on Sammie's other side and next to Maudy. Rick was at the side of their round table nearest the door and opposite Oscar, and Derek was between him and Penny.

A wait person entered, tall, skinny, crewcut, glasses, wearing jeans and sport shirt with flowers that made Penny think of Hawaii. They took a few minutes to look over the menu. Penny and Maudy chose the spinach quiche, Sammie and Oscar elected to have chicken soup with cabbage and thin noodles. Kenneth and Rick said they'd try the Southern rice with chopped pecans. Derek chose the sweet potato, white bean, and pepper casserole. The house salad and warm sour dough bread came with their meals. Oscar also ordered two bottles of the house Chablis after checking with everyone. When their wait person left, Derek said, "Oscar, I can't let you pay for Sammie and me."

"Because I'm a suspect?" Oscar was tense again.

"Because it's standard during an investigation. I can't let any of you pay for our meal. Please don't take offense."

Oscar did look offended. Sammie said, "When this awful case is over, we'd be more than happy to be wined and dined and have you to our home, too. This is a neat gathering. We should do this again when Cathy can join us."

"Definitely," said Maudy quietly, and the tense moment passed.

Penny was watching Oscar. Was he ready to let go of what had bothered him about Derek? She was seeing him in a new light. He was rather prickly and quick to react. She reacted so slowly that, if someone had been rude, she might not notice until later. Or if someone made a smart remark that begged for a quick retort, it might be hours later before she had figured out what she wanted to say. Oscar not only had quick retorts, but he had very high standards for other people's behavior, probably because he had such high standards for his own.

Sammie brought things back to a more comfortable place by reminding Oscar of the question Derek had asked. "How would you choose students for Derek to interview, Oscar?"

Oscar frowned at Penny, who smiled back, and then said to Derek. "It's rather tricky. The administration is unhappy with me. When they were so eager to hire me, they didn't realize they were getting a boat rocker. So you'd best avoid mentioning my name. But we know that drug sales are rampant here. The kids tell me it's very open. Sales go down right in front of the student union as well as in the dorms."

"I'm seeing that, too," said Kenneth. "There's a lot of marijuana being smoked in the men's dorms."

"I'd begin with students we know are selling drugs," continued Oscar. "But you'll have to make it clear that you're not the drug squad; just asking questions because of the Provost's death to get the bigger picture about life on this campus–that idea."

"Can you and Kenneth give me names?"

"Oh, yes, sadly," said Oscar. His eyes were on Penny as if she were the only other person there. "Terence Jackson and Ronny Glover, for starters."

Penny nodded.

Kenneth said, "I agree. They're some of the lads I've already talked with. Perhaps, Derek, I could interview them informally?"

"I'd like to do it formally, Kenneth, but thanks. How best to do that? You don't think the President will cooperate?"

Rick said, "She hasn't much choice if she's serious about helping you find Audrey White's killer."

"I wonder if either of those boys has ever been called before the Dean of Men," said Sammie. "Obie told us Terence was in a fight, right? Surely he had to see the Dean after that. I know they do get strict about fights. I had a student who'd been in a fight and was told he couldn't go to class for three weeks and would be sent home if it happened again."

"Three weeks is a little harsh, isn't it?" asked Penny. "What do they do with themselves for three weeks if they can't go to class?"

Sammie rolled her eyes. "Another problem. But I could find out about Terence and Ronny--I know the Dean of Men–if those two have been to his office. He's a good guy. He could call them in, and you could see them that way, Derek."

Derek considered this. "I think that might work. Thanks, everybody. This college is a mystery to me, how things actually work."

"You're not the only one," said Oscar. "We all feel that way." He smiled at Derek as their wait person reappeared with their orders.

They were leaving the restaurant at about two-thirty, Rick and Kenneth leading and Penny walking last with Oscar and Maudy, when she glimpsed Professor Clarkson sitting with Blanche Rowan of the English faculty, she whom Oscar had said was one of his problems, at a table near the window that overlooked Hillsborough Street. They were staring at her and Oscar in a very unfriendly way. "There's Professor Rowan, Oscar, over there with Clarkson."

Oscar glanced where she pointed and quickly looked away. The couple did, too. Once he'd paid for all the lunches but the Hargraves' and they were back outside on the sidewalk, he said quietly, "Blanche Rowan, my nemesis."

"What exactly makes her your nemesis?"

"She's the only tenured faculty member in English, and she hates me."

"Why? You're trying to raise the standards, make it better."

"I don't know why, Penny. She has opposed everything I've done for no reason. She has tenure, but she does diddly squat for the department. The students find her boring and can't figure out her grading system. They say she's inconsistent and unpredictable. I've spoken to her about it. I've tried everything. She has also led the move among the full-time faculty not to come to department meetings."

"I didn't know it was that bad. That makes your job pretty hard."

"Impossible," he said.

Maudy added, "He tried hard to bring her on board last fall, but she would have none of it. She's quite set in her ways."

They'd caught up to Kenneth and Rick, who were waiting at the corner for them.

"I had no choice but to give Blanche low marks on her annual faculty evaluation," added Oscar. "It made her furious, and she hasn't gotten over it. She'll never forgive me, and look at her chosen companion to hang around with, that idiot Clarkson."

Nine

Thursday, February 22. Penny had just gotten up from the table Thursday evening to make a fresh pot of tea and serve the egg custard she'd made with their share of Leroy's eggs, when someone knocked. Kenneth set down the dishes he was carrying on the counter by the sink. "I'll get it."

Delois Warren walked in, smiling, Obie behind her. "This a bad time? You're eating?"

"It's so good to see you, Delois, Obie," Kenneth said. "We've eaten. We were getting ready to have tea and Penny's egg custard." He pulled out two chairs. "Won't you join us?"

"I dearly love a good egg custard," Delois exclaimed. "If you're sure? Obie's home tonight, and he wanted to consult with you and Miss Penny." She sat down when Kenneth gestured her to a chair.

Penny was very fond of this young couple and felt touched that they'd come to consult. They were both slender with short Afros. Although Obie was muscular in a more obvious way, Delois had played girls' basketball in high school and college and worked on keeping trim and in shape. She had told Penny she still loved a good game of pick up.

"I could have talked to you on campus, Mr. Kenneth and Miss Penny, but I never seem to have a free minute."

Obie sat down, too, and Penny put bowls of custard in front of them, then for her and Kenneth.

"I never do either," Kenneth agreed, "but I'm lucky enough to have tonight off. I did an early shift today and finished at one, after the convocation crowd had cleared out. "What's up? We're happy to share any thoughts we have, but we're both so new to St. Francis that I'm not certain how much we can help you."

"Oh, you're a huge help, Mr. Kenneth, you and Miss Penny both. You might have some ideas that will help me. It's about their studies. I have a study hall for my boys most nights, and I have a senior watching them when I can't be there. I've given them progress reports, which they should give to you to sign on Tuesday, Miss Penny, with their grades so far.

"I've been checking their homework, but they keep copying. I finally figured out where they're getting the answers. Another boy has a used book with the answers written in it. Derry's a good student and knows when it's the wrong answer, but the others don't. They've been copying that book. I told Derry to erase all the answers and not to loan out his book any more. I tell them all that copying gonna get them Fs, that you strict, and they can't play no ball next fall if they don't make Cs this spring. Only it goes in one ear and out the other. So I sat down with them, one at a time, to work through their English assignment. Miss Penny, Terence can't read good and neither can Ronny. They can't read the questions they 'posed to answer, never mind the story they 'posed to read first. What good are the notes to explain the hard words if they can't read the easy words? What I'm gonna do wid 'em?"

Penny felt the same dismay she'd felt when she realized how nearly illiterate Merilee was, and here were two more of her students in the same boat. Kenneth and Obie were both waiting for her response.

"How do they get out of high school, Miss Penny?" asked Delois, throwing up her hands. "Riverdell graduates can read. We don't all go to college, but if we did, we'd do better than that. We can't graduate our high school if we don't pass all our classes and all those big tests we have to take now. I don't get it."

"It's a problem," said Penny, taking a spoonful of custard. It had turned out well. She had done it in a very slow oven, and the fresh eggs and slow cooking gave it a silky texture. She was glad she'd made two pans. This one would be gone in no time.

While Penny was trying to think what to say, Kenneth volunteered. "It's no surprise they can't concentrate. The lads I've been getting to know have a lot on their minds-- family, for one thing. Then there's marijuana. It's nothing like university when I was a student. It's a wonder they give any thought to their studies."

"This custard is some delicious, Miss Penny," said Obie, smiling broadly at her.

"Thanks. It's Leroy's fresh eggs that do it. Obie, Kenneth is right, but I don't know what to tell you or why these students have been admitted when they can barely read. It seems cruel to me to give them the hope of a college education, or as Ronny says, 'to walk across the stage and get his certificate,' when there's no way they can do the work or catch up to college level."

"But how do they get through high school, Miss Penny?" persisted Delois. She started to wave her hands but glanced at Obie and sat on them instead.

Kenneth was shaking his head as Penny said, "I know Merilee is learning disabled so she was in special education classes all through school. She's from Camden, as are Ronny and Terence. Something's different from our North Carolina school system, but I don't understand it either. It's so sad. They'll all fail, no two ways about it."

"Coach say he can get them tutoring," Obie said. "They good ball players, but their grades …"

Penny knew how hard Obie was trying to build his team, but how to catch them up when they were this far behind? "They'd need a lot of help, Obie. A good tutor would help some, but they have a lot they have to do, too. When you work with them, do they seem to be catching on? Are they trying to learn?"

Obie looked at her earnestly. "I never did tutoring, but they don't focus. They want the answers without, you know, thinking. They won't use the brains God give them. Then they bug me for the answer so they can write it down and be done. When I tell them to think, they guess wild."

"I'm seeing that, too," said Penny.

At that moment the phone rang. Kenneth walked over to their small living room and picked it up. "Sarah, good to hear from you. How's Seb? Yes, she's here. I'll put your mom on. Come see us."

Penny learned quickly that Sarah wanted her to babysit again. When Penny explained that they had company, and it wasn't a good night, Sarah said angrily, "You're always busy."

"Not always," said Penny, "but right now. This isn't a good night, and you didn't give me much notice."

Sarah slammed the phone down.

When Penny returned to the table, Kenneth raised his eyebrows. They'd talk later. Penny turned to Delois. "More tea, anyone?"

"We need to be going," said Obie. "I'm exhausted. Delois had a hard day, too."

"Let Coach Cox get them a tutor, Obie. You keep doing what you're doing and making sure they do their own work. Help them think out the answers. I think both Terence and Ronny have the intelligence to learn to read, but somehow they've been sliding by, not learning what they need to. First they have to stop copying. Sadly, Merilee is really unable to read any better than she does, I'm afraid."

As they were making their adieus, the phone rang again. Penny picked it up, while Kenneth walked down with the Warrens. Mrs. Taylor again, apologizing for slamming down the phone that morning. "Don't worry about it, Mrs. Taylor, but I want to help Merilee, if I can. You and I need to work together on this. If you do her homework for her, Merilee can't learn the skills I'm teaching her."

"Please call me Irene. I just want Merilee to graduate is all, Miss Weaver. She has her heart set on it. She made Cs, and some Bs and As in high school. I don't understand what's wrong now. She made two As last semester down there in music and history. Then she failed reading and math."

"There's a big problem, I'm afraid, Mrs. Taylor … Irene. She, in fact, should probably have failed history, but

I've learned from my chairman, Dr. Farrell, to whom Merilee talked, that her history professor, Dr. Clarkson, gave her that A in exchange for having sex with him."

Silence.

"Irene?"

"I'm here. I was afraid of something like that the way she talked about that history teacher. She said she'd be getting an A for sure because he liked her, and that was even before the final. I told her to stay away from the boys, to focus on her studies. I didn't think those teachers down there was a problem."

Penny decided that she was not the one to tell Irene about Ronny. What do you say to the mother of a brain-damaged child who is determined that her daughter will graduate from college? She couldn't think of a single thing.

Irene continued: "At least we had her tubes tied. She's so naive. I was afraid she'd get pregnant in high school. But, Miss Weaver, what can I do to help her get through your class? She needs to pass."

Penny had no answer. It sounded like Merilee's mother was hardly worried at all about her daughter's sex life and quite preoccupied with her getting a college degree, which was beyond hopeless. She said, "A good tutor may help, Irene, but Merilee needs to do her own work. I'll talk to my chairman, Dr. Farrell, and see what he suggests."

"I've already talked to Dr. Farrell," she said. "He says that Merilee isn't ready for college, but then why did the college take her?"

Why, indeed, thought Penny.

As Kenneth came back through the door, the phone rang again. Penny expected it to be Sarah, trying a different tack, more politely this time, but it was Malvina.

"Penny, have you heard anything about a big student protest scheduled for next Tuesday?"

"No, but this is only my second week. Very few students talk to me outside of class."

"Letitia does, she said."

"Yes, she and Lashandra, and Sheila, and Obie, of course."

"The others will come around, Penny."

"I think so. I hope so. But tell me what's up. A protest? I'm surprised it hasn't happened before." Penny settled on the couch, kicked off her shoes, and put her feet on the coffee table. She glanced at Kenneth, who had set about washing the dishes. Whenever she cooked, he did the washing up. He turned at the word *protest* and raised his eyebrows. She nodded to him.

"Letitia just left here. She says Rick's speech got them all fired up. Some of them got together this evening and talked about all the things they're angry about. Letitia is Merilee's roommate, and Lashandra and Sheila are roommates in the same dorm, Horton. Other girls got into the conversation, and they want to do something about Merilee and the trick that Clarkson professor played on her. Then the dorms are filthy, and most of them haven't received their scholarship money. They have a long list of grievances."

"I've heard about all those things, and I'm glad they'll fuss, Malvina. What can I do?"

"Don't be too hard on them if they miss class. I'm so pleased this generation can get into a good protest. I was in my twenties when the Civil Rights Movement took off, and we'd waited far too long for that. 'Bout time these young people took a hand in writing their own destiny."

"Right," said Penny. "It can only do good. I'll have to hold class, but I won't fail them for missing one class." She laughed. "Wish I could join 'em. So much is not right, Malvina, at St. Francis." She told her about Merilee's mother and about Obie's worry over his football boys and their near illiteracy.

"Do what you can, Penny, and Obie, too. We can't solve it all, but we might lift up a few of them and get them traveling a better road."

"I'll try," Penny said. "People talk about saving the earth and its creatures, about ecological balance. I'd like to save these young black students. This waste of human beings like I see happening at this college gets me down. Talk about an endangered species. Merilee is a gifted singer but totally at a loss with college subjects except for chorus. But her mother wants her to have a college degree."

"She wants the best for her child is all," said Malvina.

"What she's doing is throwing her to wolves like Clarkson," said Penny. "Are Letitia and the others sure Merilee is okay with what they want to do?"

"Oh, yes, very much so. I feel protective of her, too, Penny, but why shouldn't she carry her troubles onto a larger stage and call attention to the racket your college profs and some in power have going with these inadequately prepared students?"

Penny couldn't argue with that.

~

Tuesday morning was clear and sunny with the temperature rising steadily and predicted to reach seventy-five degrees. Oscar walked into Penny's classroom about eight-thirty just as the last three students decided to take their F for missing one class period and went out the door to join the protest outside. Penny was watching out her fourth floor window the milling students in front of Booher Hall. She had picked out Lashandra with a bull horn and Sheila beside her. They, Merilee, Ronnie, Terence, and most of the others hadn't showed up at all for the eight o'clock.

When Penny arrived with Sammie a little after seven, all had been quiet on campus, but around eight, she could hear voices outside, penetrating even to the fourth floor, and instead of students hurrying down the halls to get to class on time, those already in the building seemed to be leaving as fast as they arrived. She had written on the board that she would hold class as usual, and those not there would receive an F for that day's work, but she told the half-dozen who turned up that there was apparently a student protest in the works, and they could certainly go, if they didn't mind getting an F, which wouldn't count that much overall. They didn't mind and left.

Oscar walked over to the window. Penny wished he wouldn't stand quite so close. She was determined to keep their connection from becoming sexual. "So they've done it," he said. "Thank God. They might pull off what no other earthly or heavenly power seemed able to."

"What's that exactly?" Penny was watching Lashandra speaking through the bullhorn. The crowd had quieted.

"Getting rid of Christine Siler. Do these windows open?"

"I have no idea."

"The ones in my office are sealed." Oscar pulled a lower window's handle toward him, and it came open. The chilly air moved into the room, but it was far too warm anyway. "Do you mind? Are you warm enough?"

"Oh, yes. Listen, my students are the ring leaders. Lashandra is talking to the crowd. Sheila and Letitia are there, too, and they've got Merilee with them."

"They should have left Merilee out of it. She won't understand."

"I agree, but it's too late now."

They could hear Lashandra. Her words faded out some, but the gist was clear. "We've had enough," she declaimed. "Merilee, my friend, was took advantage of by a professor."

"Who?" someone yelled.

"Clarkson," yelled Sheila, who had a strong, carrying voice. She took the megaphone from Lashandra, and her words came through clearly. "We been suckered, is what. Our dorm rooms is filthy. We got roaches. They ain't been cleaned in years, maybe since this place was founded in 1867."

There was a ripple of excited laughter.

"We don't want to live in no pigsty, eat no nasty pig food. And we need our money. They got our money, and they ain't give it to us. That President Siler got all our money, drives around in her big black Chrysler, and we ain't got shit."

Lashandra got the megaphone back and yelled, more assertively now, "We got questions. We want answers. We got questions. We want answers." Then the crowd took up the chant.

Oscar shut the window and turned to Penny. "Thank God. They've done it."

He put his arm around Penny's shoulder as they turned away from the window. Penny wished he wouldn't embrace her. She moved to go to her desk and pack up her books before he could kiss her. She glanced at the window in the door to the classroom and saw a familiar face. Was it Blanche Rowan? She thought so. That grey hair set in a soft perm, dark-framed glasses, blue eyes. Who else? Had Blanche seen Oscar hug her? He apparently hadn't seen Blanche or didn't care.

"I'd rather be out there with the kids," he said. "I was at NCCU in the '60s, worked with SNIC in the summers doing voter registration in the deep South. I was beginning to think this new generation had no sense of history. All they wanted was fast cars, expensive clothes, big houses, to play for NFL or NBA, fat chance. They can't seem to see the point of using their brains, for God's sake. All they talk about is basketball or football and nothing else. I'd about given up on them."

Penny erased the board and turned to pick up her backpack. "I wouldn't write these kids off yet. Rick is hopeful we can make a difference here, and according to Malvina, Letitia's aunt, Rick's speech at the convocation is what set off this protest. I'm going to work in the Writing Center until my 10 a.m. seminar, but I doubt I'll have any students coming by. Maybe Obie. I'll see you later then."

She walked toward the door. She could tell he wanted to talk more, but with Blanche Rowan roaming the halls, spying? She would prepare for her Thursday classes, get that done.

She didn't see Oscar again until her seminar had ended and she was back in the Writing Center. There were no students to consult her, but it was quiet, and she could work.

Her students, even Lashandra and Letitia, to her surprise, had come to the seminar. They brought the news that Acting Provost Grubb had sent word by his secretary that all students on athletic scholarships would lose them if they were involved at all in the protest. Since many students, men and women, had those scholarships, it broke up the protest, but Lashandra said they were going to do a special issue of the campus paper, *The Winged Messenger,* and tell everybody the truth. "This here college got a lot to learn about telling the truth," Lashandra said. Penny had smiled. Obie seemed worried and distracted. He probably hadn't had any input into the Coach's and the Provost's decision to use their scholarships as a weapon, but he apparently didn't feel that he could join the complaints the others expressed at some length about how unfair that had been.

"We got issues," said Letitia. "You'd think they'd remember all we achieved in the '60s by standing up for what's right. They keep on telling us to remember our history and be grateful to our ancestors for the civil rights they fought for, but they've forgotten how it all happened. They're just into their money and their big cars. We got to spoil their little game. A special issue of the paper should do it."

Penny remembered how happy Letitia and Lashandra had looked, full of their new roles as protest leaders, their eyes bright, their whole bodies energized and fully alive. Nothing like a fight against injustice to revitalize the whole human being and give these young students a sense of purpose.

Penny had smiled at them and let them talk for half an hour before steering them back to their autobiographies. Obie was relieved when they took up their writing again and offered to read. Penny was sure he would find a way to reconcile his sympathy for the protest and his loyalty to Coach Cox. She suspected that Obie thought Cox and the Provost, no doubt with the President's support, had made a bad mistake.

Oscar walked into the Writing Center at eleven-thirty. Penny was reading Obie's autobiography and was totally immersed in it when he came and stood before her and said, "Is it well written?"

Penny jumped and then saw it was Oscar. "Sorry, what did you say?"

"Is it well written?"

"Oh, yes, given that it's his first creative writing class. It's Obie Warren's. He's Assistant Football Coach. He had quite a rough childhood. It makes me even more proud of him than I already was."

What did Oscar want of her now? He sat down in a desk near her and said, "Tell me about his work."

"His mother was a drug addict, and his father divorced her when Obie was six. Then Obie became her caretaker, making sure she ate, finding her when she didn't come home at night, stealing money from her purse when she had passed out and going to buy groceries or his school supplies, whatever they needed. This went on until he was twelve and finally got her into detox. The social services people never found out. He did such a good job that few people understood the load he was carrying, and those

few who did helped him out rather than turning him in to
social services. Amazing. Now he's such a good,
conscientious adult. I stand in awe."

Oscar smiled at her. "Not a unique story," he said.
"Listen, Penny. I've had a phone call from Siler. You won't
believe this. She blames *me* for the protest."

Ten

Tuesday, February 27. The faculty dining room was practically empty when Penny and Sammie entered at a little before one o'clock that Tuesday. "I think they close pretty soon," Sammie said, picking up a plastic tray and silverware wrapped in a paper napkin. "Oh, goodie, they still have barbecued ribs left. Afternoon, Miss Rosa. Ribs, please, macaroni and string beans."

"Afternoon, Miss Sammie, and Miss … I'm sorry, I forgot your name. You're Mr. Kenneth's wife. I remember that."

"I'm Penny, and I'll have the ribs, the mashed potatoes and beans, too."

"Mr. Kenneth so nice to everybody," said Rosa as she filled their plates and passed them over. "He gets us laughing, too. Need to laugh sometimes over what these students get up to."

"Protests?" Sammie set her plate on her tray and hesitated. "What did you think of it, Rosa?"

"It don't make me no never mind." Rosa's eyes searched the rest of the room and glanced at the tall man a few yards away, serving desserts. "We had to go as guards. We ain't had no protest here since I been here. Fifteen year in April."

"They were noisy," said Sammie, "but they didn't do any harm. Protests are healthy compared to the drugs, sex, and fast cars these kids get up to. Not to mention those clubs all over Raleigh that draw them like flies."

"Yes, ma'am, and they drunk, too, when they come on back to they dorm way late."

"You'd rather see them in protests, wouldn't you, Miss Rosa, than falling down drunk, getting in fights, all that?"

Again Rosa looked around the room, with a glance to her cohort. "I don't like to see 'em drunk, Miss Sammie, no, ma'am. But I don't know about no protest. The President told us to 'rest 'em if they gots rowdy."

"Did you arrest anyone?" asked Sammie. She hadn't moved, and the dessert man was fidgeting.

"Only one girl. After Dr. Grubb's secretary spoke, that Green girl what's always showing off started in making fun of the President and Dr. Grubb, and we tol' her to give over the bullhorn, and she ain't. So we ain't had no choice but to 'rest her. The Wake cops took her downtown to cool off."

"Sheila," said Penny.

Sammie shook her head and went on to the antsy dessert man. They were the last, and the servers must have wanted to clean up. Sammie took lemon meringue pie. So did Penny. It was one of her favorites. She followed Sammie to the far corner. She thought Rosa and the dessert man looked relieved when they'd paid and settled down to eat.

Sammie unloaded her tray and took Penny's, too, to add to the stack on a side table. "You want iced tea?" Penny nodded, and Sammie fetched a pitcher and two glasses with ice. She sat down and rearranged her dishes before saying anything. "This stinks. Sheila Green's one of your freshmen?"

"Yes, and I've gotten fond of her. She gave me fits the first day, but she settled down and is working hard now. A drama major. I like her spirit. She's Lashandra's roommate and wanted to do the creative writing course, but her advisor wouldn't let her. She enjoys fighting with authority figures, but that might make her a good leader. I was watching this morning. She and Lashandra were on the bullhorn. She's a natural—clear, strong, convincing. She'll be okay, Sammie. It will take more than a night in jail to quench her spirit."

"Oh, I'm not worried about her spirit," Sammie said in a low voice. Today she was in red with scarlet poppies on her short-sleeved blouse. She had removed her suit jacket and kicked off her red heels under the table. She had a short Afro, and red earrings shaped like poppies dangled from her ears. "I'm worried about this damn college. When they take in smart ones who could achieve and have real potential as future leaders, these kids don't have a snowball's chance in hell of getting support and encouragement from the top. The President has no concept, none of those bigwigs do. It's shitty, Penny. Sheila has you, but who else sees what she could be, what her gifts are?"

"Maybe one adult who sees and appreciates her is enough for this one," said Penny. "Remember, she's a very spirited young woman. She'll make it, I think. She has had support in the past. She's very confident."

Sammie picked up one of her ribs. "I'm more worried about all the others who are intelligent and capable whom nobody sees accurately. It's such a waste. You, I, Oscar, Obie, a few others. We can't win against this tide of shit, Penny."

"Oh, I understand. These young people, I begin to see, are an endangered species."

Sammie nodded. "You got it in one, girlfriend, but there's other bad stuff, too. So here's you and here's Oscar, both doing your damnedest to help the kids." She put down her ribs and wiped her fingers on a napkin.

"By the way, Siler now blames Oscar for the protest," said Penny.

"She does? Stupid bitch," Sammie said in a low voice. "They're so off base. They can't even save their own skins. Oscar could do that for them, if they'd let him alone. But it gets worse, Penny. You heard the gossip about you and Oscar?"

Penny flashed on Blanche's face in her classroom door's window. She shook her head and suddenly felt a great sense of dread.

"Word is that you and Oscar are having an affair."

Penny's first thought was that Kenneth would hear the rumor and go berserk. "We aren't," she said to Sammie. She pushed her plate away and pulled over the lemon pie. The dessert man was back in the room and took their plates. He fussed with the table where the condiments were, and then he disappeared back into the kitchen.

Sammie waited until they were alone. "I knew that. I know how much you love Kenneth. The gossip mill around here is atrocious. They'll crucify you soon as look at you."

The pie looked delicious, but Penny now had no appetite. "I like Oscar a lot," she started. Should she tell Sammie how flirtatious he was?

"Of course," said Sammie, taking a forkful of pie. "Who but an idiot wouldn't? He cares, he works his tail off. He protects his faculty. He'll be livid, I know that. Are you worried?"

"A little," said Penny. "To be honest, more than a little. Oscar treats me really well, consults me when I have no idea how to advise him. He likes to know what I think."

"No crime in that, Penny. Eat your pie. They're trying to close up."

"I'm not hungry." Penny pushed her pie away. "Sorry."

Sammie got up and retrieved a take-out box from the side table. She slid Penny's pie into it, closed the top, and handed it to her. "Come on, let's go. We can't talk in here, anyway." She slipped back into her lively red shoes and jacket, and Penny put her sweater back on and hung her purse over her shoulder.

As they pushed out of the dining room door, the dessert man locked it behind them.

"We'll go back to my office," Sammie said. "You left your books there. My colleagues have classes until two-thirty, so nobody will bother us. No wonder Oscar talks to you, Penny. You have so much common sense."

"Sometimes I wonder." Penny was thinking that maybe she had no real place at this college. How could she, as a white woman, no matter how much she wanted to help and cared now about Sheila, Letitia, and the rest of them, actually do any good? A phrase her son Ted used to say when a child came to her. She felt like a "gunshotter shot down." Hadn't Oscar tried to warn her that it was hopeless here? The corruption at the top would win. He had called St. Francis a sinking ship. She'd wanted to argue with him then, but maybe he was right. "Oscar thinks this place is a sinking ship," she said. "Do you? But how can I help? Won't this rumor destroy any good I could do? Besides, he does sometimes hug me. He's affectionate and impulsive. I like him, but I think Blanche Rowan saw him hug me this morning when we were watching the protest from the windows of my classroom."

"Oh, pooh, Blanche is nothing. Nobody listens to her. Ignore her. Ignore the rumor. No telling what they say about me, Penny. I'll stick here and be a burr in their butts as long as I can, and then I'll go to a decent college and take the talented students in history with me. Don't quit over something this stupid, Penny. So he hugs you. So? He hugs everybody he likes. He hugs me, too. Ignore it, Penny. I told you so it wouldn't catch you by surprise. You're my girlfriend, right?"

Penny looked at Sammie and her serious eyes, the beginning of a smile on her lips. It helped. Sammie was her source of common sense, Sammie and Kenneth.

"Of course, Sammie. It's just ..."

"What 'just'?"

"Kenneth. He gets jealous easily, and he's already suspicious of Oscar. He thought Oscar killed the Provost and got upset when I said that was impossible. Oscar raged, but he didn't kill."

"That's Kenneth's problem," announced Sammie as they reached the back door to Booher Hall. "Derek's got his problems, too. You gotta stay sane. That's your best suit."

"Even when I feel wobbly?" asked Penny as they reached the elevator and Sammie pushed the up button.

When the elevator arrived, Merilee stepped off. "Oh, Miz Weaver, I been trying to find you."

Sammie said, "I'll be in my office, Penny. Come on up after you've talked to her, or bring her with you?"

Merilee shook her head, so Sammie let the door close. The basement hall was deserted. There were only a few classrooms on this level and some faculty offices. A large room at the other end of the hall was a computer lab where students could type and print their papers or check their email.

"What's up, Merilee?"

Even though she had been the focus of the protest only hours earlier, Merilee looked the same--soft, defenseless and innocent, which she was in some hard-to-explain way. But she couldn't seem to find the words now that she had Penny's full attention.

Merilee stared at the floor, the old and faded linoleum, cracked in places, with ground-in dirt near the walls. "Miz Weaver, I know you give us an F when we miss class, but I can't help it sometimes."

When she lifted her head, she looked frightened.

Penny spoke gently. "You mean about the protest this morning?"

"No, ma'am. You said one F won't hurt us, and we all went to the protest. Letitia say I have to go with her and Lashandra and Sheila. They say you not mad around that."

"No, Merilee."

"But, see, you said if we leave early for spring break and miss Thursday class, we get another F. That's two Fs, Miz Weaver."

"Then come to class Thursday, Merilee."

"I can't."

"Why not?"

"'Cause of my ride home. See, I ride with Terence. He say give you this note." Merilee handed Penny a torn sheet of lined notebook paper folded over.

Terence had written: "Miz Weaver, I gotta go home tonite. My boy got kilt and his funeral bees tamarra. This bees my exkuzed note. Terence M. Jackson."

Interesting timing, thought Penny. She knew they were allowed excused absences for family deaths. They could bring a funeral program as their excused note. A "boy" was a close friend, but was a friend's funeral a legitimate excuse? "Terence had better to talk to me himself, Merilee, but I can't excuse you, in any case. You can't afford to miss any classes." Of course, she wouldn't be able to learn in them, and yet it seemed necessary to Penny that she preserve the discipline she was trying to establish, admittedly, so far, with limited success.

"My mama say tell you it's my onliest ride. I havta go, Miz Weaver. I ain't got no other ride. Me and Ronny gonna ride with Terence when that policeman's done talking to him."

"What policeman?"

"I don't know his name. Terence tol' Ronny he had to talk to him on account of that lady got killed, you know?"

"The Provost?"

"Yes, ma'am. Terence, he say the man be crazy, but soon as he done talking, we be driving to Camden. He ain't got time to talk to you. It's why I brung his note for you."

"I see. I think you'll all be getting Fs, but have your mother call me, Merilee. She knows my number."

"Yes, ma'am." Penny watched Merilee walk in her careful, deliberate way over to the outer door and push it open with her hip, then go out into the warm sunshine. Suddenly Penny felt unutterably weary.

~

Penny was relaxing Tuesday evening after supper, reading an Elizabeth George novel. Spring break, which began on the following Friday, might even give her a chance to finish it. She had asked Sammie to drop her at Food Plus, where the bookmobile parked Tuesday afternoon. She was going to walk home from there, but Sammie joined her, found a Toni Morrison novel she hadn't read yet, and then they drove on to Penny's.

Sammie had urged her to say anything she wanted to about the rumor or Oscar, or Merilee, or anything else. "We don't want to lose you, girl. You know we each hold up a place in this world, and other people depend on us to keep holding our place as best we can for as long as we can. Maybe you've only been at St. Francis a few weeks …"

"Two weeks," said Penny.

"… but you've got your place with me, Oscar, Obie, with your students. We need you."

Penny felt bleak. "Thanks, Sammie, but I think I have to work through this on my own."

"We been through too much," Sammie said. "We fought nuclear power and formaldehyde, and we had that awful election. Don't quit on us, Penny. You got friends."

"I know." When Sammie stopped in the driveway at 7 Whitfield Mill Road, Penny hugged her. "You're a wonderful friend. I don't know why this is getting me down so much. I'll work it through." She managed a half-hearted smile. "Thanks for all your support." Penny opened the car door.

"You got it, any time. You'll call?"

"I'll call. I'm funny, I guess. Sometimes I want to be by myself."

So she had been. She'd written in her diary and figured out that what was worrying her most was Kenneth. The rumor was wrong, but she had come to care about Oscar more than she had about any man since she'd met Kenneth ten years earlier. She didn't want to feel what she was feeling for Oscar, and she didn't know what to do about it. If Oscar had simply been a good friend, she could have laughed the whole thing off with Kenneth as a stupid rumor. But there was that grain of truth. She could hardly tell Kenneth that she was attracted to Oscar even though she didn't want to be. She hadn't been able to tell anyone else either--not Sammie, and she didn't think Cathy would understand. They would both try, but they were part of the world she and Kenneth were in together. She and Kenneth were a team. She wanted them to be a team. She wanted their friends to see them that way.

Blessedly, the phone didn't ring. Sarah didn't call. Kenneth didn't get off until eleven. She ate a simple supper of poached eggs on toast with a cut up orange for her "vegetable," and settled to her novel afterwards with a pot of tea.

She didn't know the answer, didn't know what to do, but at least she knew what was bothering her underneath everything else, like a splinter buried so deep it was hard to reach with a needle, much less get out. It hurt. It didn't stop hurting. She'd have to live with it.

She was caught up in the George and happily forgetting everything else when a car drove in. Formy crowed, and car doors slammed. Voices. Malvina? Must be. Then Sammie's.

She shuffled into her slippers and went to turn on the porch light. She opened the door to Malvina, Sammie and Letitia, who said, "Ms. Weaver, we need your help." Penny waved them in. "If I can," she said. "What's up?"

Eleven

Tuesday, February 27. Once they'd settled in the living room part of their small apartment, and Penny had emptied the teapot for the others and put the kettle on for a fresh pot, Letitia said, "It's about the protest, Miss Penny. Can I call you that?"

"Of course." Penny couldn't help smiling. Letitia was such a complex package, respectful and yet impudent all at the same time. She was looking sexy tonight, as usual, in a long-sleeved, vee-neck orange tee shirt that showed off her cleavage; but she was bright and perky, her brown eyes intense and totally focused on Penny. Clearly something was on her mind beyond the ordinary. Penny glanced at Sammie, who merely smiled and nodded. Was this a plot to reinforce what Sammie had said that afternoon, that she had a place at St. Francis? Letitia was acting as if Penny were really needed. Even if it was a plot, it felt good. She loved to give advice, but few asked for it, and her own children hardly ever.

"See, Miss Penny, we're so frustrated. We had that protest, and it went so well. I mean, I don't think any students went to their eight o'clocks. They all came, and some who never get up early got up for that. Then the new Provost broke it up, telling us we could lose our scholarships. Most of the serious students are on athletic scholarships. I'm not. I have a scholarship from the United

Negro College Fund, but maybe they'll take that, too." She looked at Malvina, who shook her head, her face solemn.

"Aunt Malvie doesn't think they'd dare, but so far the administrators have acted pretty stupid, right? Everything we listed in our grievances that we gave to the President is a real problem, and I don't know any serious student who isn't unhappy here. Hey, we came here to get an education. So what's all this shit about professors trading sex for As? They keep the lawn mowed. We see a whole slew of landscapers out there every day, mowing, blowing leaves off the sidewalks, planting flowers, but they got no money to kill the roaches in our dorms? We eat bad food, and we can't even get our scholarship money so we can go buy a burger sometimes if we want to. It's downright shameful."

"You were going to do a special issue of *The Winged Messenger*, weren't you?" asked Penny.

"We were, but the word came down from President Siler that we can't do that. There's no money, and anyway, they'll censor it. Their office has to approve every issue. Siler sent word to our counselor in Horton Dorm that she'll meet with the protest leaders Thursday, but we know she ain't gonna do shit anyway. They already killed the protest."

"I don't know about that," said Penny. "Of course, as I've learned the hard way, when you pick up a weapon, your opponent may well pick up one, too. So you started the protest, and they tried to stop it by putting on economic pressure." Penny saw that Malvina and Sammie were smiling, regarding her with immense satisfaction, and she had to admit that it was fun to plot protest strategy with Letitia.

"That's why we're here," Letitia said. "Aunt Malvie said you'd had a lot of experience with protests and might have some ideas about what to do next."

"What were you yourself thinking of doing since the student newspaper idea folded?"

"Going to the local papers, I guess, *The Moon* in Durham and the *News and Observer* in Raleigh."

"Good thinking. One idea I got from Erik Erikson, the psychiatrist, was to know your counterplayer. Who is that, do you think?"

"President Siler?"

"I think so. As far as the protest goes, what is her goal?"

"To shut it down?"

"Yes, but why? Why not just spend a little more money on cleaning the dorms, providing better quality food? Why not fire Clarkson and make him an example of what not to do if you're a professor?"

"You mean, why shouldn't she give in to our demands?"

"Yes. They sound reasonable to me, and she would come off looking good."

"We want her to give in, but we don't think she ever will. You mean, why not? What is she worried about?"

Malvina's eyes were alight, and she was beaming at Letitia. Sammie had a glow on her face as she looked at Penny, as though this was exactly the kind of need Penny filled so well. It was fun, Penny thought. It felt good to be consulted, to have experience in long-term struggles. She'd certainly had enough of those, but this college was a whole new one for her, a new puzzle to solve. She must want to solve it. She was feeling quite happy now.

Letitia stared at Penny, concentrating. "She doesn't want to look bad?"

"Why would she look bad? To whom would she look bad?"

"She looks bad to us because she won't listen to us or do what is needed. It's so dumb if you're running a college to have roaches and dirty old professors and stuff. It would be very smart to fire him immediately."

"What she's doing *is* dumb," said Penny, "but she let these problems happen. You're telling her the facts, the facts she already knew, most likely. Why wouldn't she want these facts known or better known?"

"This is hard," said Letitia. "Help me, Aunt Malvie."

"You're doing great," said Malvina. "I want to hear how you reason it out. I might learn something. I always do learn from you young people."

"Siler knows," repeated Letitia, "but she doesn't want more people to know."

"Who in particular doesn't she want to know about the college's problems?" The teakettle began to whistle. Penny thought of offering more tea, but they were all so intensely focused on this discussion that she decided to wait. She leaned over from her chair and turned down the heat under the kettle.

"Students who might consider coming to St. Francis and decide not to?"

"Right. Who else?"

"Their parents? Oh, and our parents, who might not yet know how bad it is, especially that dirty old professor. Who'd want to send their daughter to a college where that kind of thing happened? My dad would be furious if that happened to me and jerk me out of here really fast."

"Excellent," said Penny. "Anyone else?"

"Other professors who might want to leave if that kind of behavior was allowed and the students mistreated?"

"Right, and we do have some good faculty here who care about the students. Now, think about it economically. Where does St. Francis get its money to run this place, pay the teachers and administrators, janitors, counselors, coaches, secretaries, kitchen staff, security guards, landscapers, and all the people who serve the students in various ways?"

"They get it from us. This place is expensive, twelve thousand a year if you live on campus."

"Yes, in fact almost all the college money comes from the students, from their government scholarships, loans, and their parents' savings. Also this President is trying to get more donations from the alumni."

"Oh, then, she wouldn't want the alumni to know either, would she?"

"Definitely not," said Sammie, unable to contain herself any longer. "Don't forget the college's board of trustees. Christine Siler was hired by them and serves at their discretion."

"Maybe this is a good moment to offer you another cup of tea?" Penny stood up. The rest of them did, too, and stretched. Penny rinsed the pot with fresh boiling water, dipped out two heaping teaspoons of Earl Grey for the pot, and refilled it.

When they'd settled again, and all had fresh cups, she said, "Christine Siler is running a business. What must a good business do to keep and expand its customers?"

"It has to give good service and get a good reputation," said Letitia. "My dad works at Sampson Pine--well, it has a new name now, but it's basically still the same company. He told me about when Sampson Pine did all that bad polluting, and the community got very upset because people were getting sick. The people in the plant knew it was bad, but they were afraid to say anything for fear they'd lose their jobs. Oh, yeah, and now we're afraid because we might lose our scholarships."

"Right," said Penny.

"But the community took it up and raised a fuss, and the owners didn't want people to have bad feelings about the company, so eventually they sold it. Too many problems for them. But it was a whole lot of other people fussing that set off the change. Then the new company bought the new, better machinery, which cut the pollution way down, ninety percent less, Daddy says."

"So then how best can you reach these groups that might have influence on President Siler that the students don't seem to have?"

"The newspapers."

"Yes, good. What other strategies?"

"We could print our own flyer or copy our list of demands and send that to our parents and maybe the alumni. I don't know how we'd get the alumni addresses though."

Malvina said, "I know several people in Shagbark who graduated from St. Francis, and they would have addresses of their friends and relatives who went there."

Sammie grinned. "I bet I could get a list of the alumni, maybe even an address list. They must send out an alumni newsletter. Someone in the administration will have it, some secretary will have the mailing list."

"They do have a newsletter, I think," said Malvina. "I'll ask my friend."

"There's email, too," said Penny. "You could email your demands to as many people as possible here and wherever your friends live. Tell them to forward it far and wide. St. Francis gets its students from up and down the East Coast and also has some from as far away as California, not to mention Africa and the Caribbean."

"Yes!" exclaimed Letitia. "This is great, Miss Penny." She jumped up as though ready to start the next stage of her crusade immediately.

"Remember though," Penny said, "they have weapons, too. Not that you can't fight back, but don't be surprised."

Malvina said, "Yes, my good friend who was at St. Francis in the '60s started a protest, and she and the other leaders were expelled, and then a letter was put in their files that other colleges would be advised not to admit them. It took some years before she could get back into college. Her parents had to threaten to sue St. Francis before they removed that letter from her file."

"Oh, no," said Letitia. "This is hard stuff, isn't it?" She looked with dismay at the women gathered around her.

"Definitely," said Sammie, "but worth the trouble. Anyway, it's how we have kept moving forward, no matter how much people tried to stop us."

Penny said, "Letitia, you have a gift for this kind of struggle and the passion to persist when it gets hard. We're with you, us old, experienced fighters." She smiled at Malvina and Sammie.

As they were leaving, all the women hugged her, Sammie last, who said, "See why we got to keep you, girl?"

The phone rang not long after the women left, about nine. Penny had been hunting through some books Oscar had loaned her for material to use to stimulate her students' next essay. She hoped to find something entirely new and interesting for them and then to hold them to her assigned topic. She would have them do several drafts in class so she would know it was their own work. Handing in essays found on the internet or borrowed from another student was endemic at this college, she was learning. She had been hearing tales she found very disturbing. Oscar said he made his students write in class. So would she. Her students would learn something if they were able to make the effort.

It was Sarah on the phone. "Mom, have you got a minute?"

"Yes."

"I'm so mad at Leroy I could scream."

"What happened?" Penny put a slip of paper in the book, closed it, and put her feet up on the coffee table. She was thinking that Leroy had every reason to be angry at Sarah.

"He's upset about not seeing Seb. He kept him tonight for a couple of hours, but he wants to see him more often. He says Seb should be able to visit him. Seb didn't help either. He cried when I took him home tonight."

"He's in bed now?"

"Yeah, Mom. It's after nine. He fell asleep in the car, zonked. But it's not like a divorce. We're not married. I don't have to do what he wants."

Penny thought, he's Seb's father, and Seb knows it, but that wouldn't go down well with Sarah. "So what will you do?"

"Brian wants me just to cut him off altogether. He says Seb will forget him."

Penny doubted that. Her first memory of her father was from when she was less than two years old.

"What do you think, Sarah? What's best for you and Seb?"

After spending that time with Letitia, it was such a contrast talking to Sarah, who did not want to know what Penny thought, who had probably called to vent her frustration, and probably couldn't think very well about her child or his feelings. Penny found she resented Brian's bossiness about Sarah's life and the way she had so recently been living it. It may not have been ideal, but it had been workable, and Leroy was the one who had especially made it work.

"I don't know, Mom. I can't see giving Leroy visitation rights. That's stupid. Brian says he has no legal right to see Seb, since we never married."

"I'm not so sure about that. Have you talked to a lawyer? Kate could tell you."

"No, Mom. I'm not going to talk to a lawyer. Couldn't you explain to Leroy that I'm trying to make a whole new life with Brian?"

"You'd better do that, be the one who explains to Leroy." She didn't say that Leroy was within his rights to want to see his son.

"Oh, Mom, you aren't helping."

Penny thought, I never seem to help you, Sarah, or at least do whatever you wish me to do. She expected Sarah to slam down the telephone. Instead, she said, "Mom, couldn't I bring Seb over to see you, and then Leroy could see him then if he wanted to?"

"I don't think that would work, Sarah. It sounds like you'd like Seb to see Leroy, but you're afraid of Brian's disapproval."

"No, I'm not. Mom, you don't understand."

Someone knocked at the door. Penny carried the phone over to the door and looked out the curtain. Leroy.

"Listen, Sarah. I've got someone at the door. Can I call you back in a little while?"

"Forget it, Mom." Then she did slam down the phone.

Penny opened the door to Leroy in his usual winter garb of cut-off jeans, a tee shirt and sneakers. His summer garb left off the tee shirt and substituted flip flops for the tennis shoes. "Come on in."

While she put the phone back, he asked, "Am I interrupting, Penny?"

"No, it's okay. The call was over. Would you like some Earl Grey tea?"

"No, maybe a glass of water. I'm on my way to bed, but I saw your light."

"What's up?" asked Penny, getting Leroy's water and her half a cup of cold tea from the coffee table and sitting across from him at the kitchen table. He wasn't one to confide or talk about his feelings, but he must be upset.

"I couldn't decide whether to talk to you or to Kate. I decided to talk to you first."

"Okay," said Penny, thinking he probably would follow her advice. What a paradox it all was. Her advice didn't vary much, but how well it went down with other people certainly did.

"It's about Seb and Sarah. Did she tell you I want to marry her now?"

Penny nodded.

"And that she wants to marry the guy she's dating? She's going to live with him. She says she doesn't need me to babysit any more." He said it mechanically as he stared at the glass of water, so far untouched. His face didn't normally reveal his feelings, but Penny knew he was hurting a lot, knew how much he loved Seb. He had lived without Sarah quite nicely, but Seb had been part of his life since infancy. He'd told her that Seb was the only truly good thing that had ever happened to him, not counting the friendship of Penny and the others living in their little neighborhood.

"Sarah told me some about it. I felt sad that she would do that to you and Seb. He loves you a lot, and you've been a good father to him."

"I should have married her. Now it's too late. She says Seb seeing me is not normal. She wants a normal life for Seb." His expression was wooden.

Penny ached for him. It was one thing Leroy couldn't do, achieve normalcy. His childhood had been too strange, and he did very well, considering how little affection he'd had from his abusive mother or the series of foster parents he'd had after he was taken from her at age five.

"You give Seb what you have to give, Leroy. You love him, and he is happy with you. Normal isn't everything. It may not even be that important." Ah, now she was taking sides, but she knew Sarah was wrong, if only Sarah herself could figure that out. She couldn't promise Leroy that Sarah would be wiser in the future. She hoped she would be. "You haven't done anything wrong, Leroy. It's a hard situation. She is trying to be a good mother, and she wants this marriage to Brian. A lot could change, but I know it's hard. Frankly, what she's doing really bothers me, but she doesn't take advice from me. I think she'll have to sort this one out herself." Which wasn't much comfort.

"I figured," he said. "Thanks, Penny. I don't know what to do, but it hurts, you know?"

"I know. It wouldn't hurt to talk to Kate, see what your legal rights are."

"No, I think I'll wait. Sarah's young still. I'll miss Seb if she doesn't bring him, but she's a good mother. He'll be okay. Only I thought I'd get to see him grow up."

Then Penny did see the hurt in his eyes. He wasn't a man you could hug. She said, giving him her whole attention and holding his eyes. "I know."

Twelve

Thursday, March 1. Sammie had cancelled her classes that Thursday before spring break, which began the next afternoon. She said so many students left early that it wasn't worth it to hold class, so Penny rode in with Obie, who had to be there whether his "boys" were or not. Penny saw few faculty or Vice President cars in the parking lot as they crossed the campus from College Avenue, where many of the staff, adjuncts and young faculty parked to avoid the parking fee.

Booher Hall was deserted. Penny had told her students she would hold class, since her students couldn't afford to miss class after getting such a late start, but she wouldn't teach new material. She would be there to answer questions and review. They'd had their midterm tests the previous Thursday, and she could go over problems they were having. She wondered if any would show up.

When she walked into classroom 402, she found Sheila Green and no one else. The room seemed huge, and Sheila looked very small and self-conscious. Her normally beautifully braided dreads looked nappy, and she wore no beads in them. In fact, she was wearing pajamas, and her light green eyes looked bloodshot. "Good morning, Sheila. I'm glad you came."

"Can I go back to the dorm, Miz Weaver? I only got out of jail yesterday afternoon, and I'm so tired. Don't look like nobody comin' nohow."

Penny set her backpack on the desk and got out her folder of English 21 and handed Sheila the day's roll sheet to sign. "I can't keep you from leaving, but you didn't do well on the midterm, and here's your chance to work on some things that are hard for you."

"What did I get for my grade?"

"A low D. It was the grammar part of the test that pulled you down. You can write well. You made a B on your essay but an F on the grammar."

"Oh, no. Shit. Sorry, Miz Weaver. My dad gonna be mad as a hornet. They had to borrow money to send me here. He's a pastor, and Mama teaches at Virginia State. She says I got to do well my freshman year. They can't afford no loan lessen I make good grades. They won't like my being in jail neither, even if they did jail time when they was young. Can I get me some extra credit?"

Sheila, for all her histrionics, was endearing. Penny hardly knew why, but she also wanted her to do well and knew she could if she worked at it.

"Extra credit won't do it, Sheila." Penny sat down on the front edge of her desk. "You should be able to pass this class with ease if you give it some serious attention."

"I know. I been so involved in that protest, I ain't been studying. I'm sorry, Miz Penny, and they didn't ought to put me in that cruel jail neither. They laughed at me, those gooks they had for prison guards. I couldn't wait to get back to my dorm. Our roaches ain't nothin' to those jail roaches."

Penny wanted to smile at this so gifted, intelligent girl with her normally sunny and friendly disposition. What could she say to cheer her up and ease her into working harder at her studies? "Tell you what. Looks like you're the only one coming. Let's work on your subject and verb agreement and some of these other grammar things that are tripping you up. You want your parents to be proud of you, and you can do the work. It ain't that hard," she added, hoping to stir Sheila out of her dumps.

Sheila laughed. "Guess you right, Miz Weaver. Okay. What did I get wrong?"

Sheila responded well. She focused in a whole new way on the problem of singular and plural in nouns and verbs. They also worked on what made a complete sentence versus a fragment or a run-on.

Penny felt lighter herself as she watched Sheila stroll out of her classroom and turn toward the elevator. Then Sheila turned back, stuck out her tongue, rolled her eyes, and said, "Thanks, Miz Weaver."

Penny laughed. Before she thought about it, she walked in the direction of the departmental office. She hadn't seen Oscar since they'd watched the protest together Tuesday morning. If she knew him at all, he would be there in his office. All the classrooms she passed were empty, and the faculty offices were closed, even the Writing Center. But the English Department office door was open, and so was Oscar's door.

She had been told once that people either run toward their fears or away from them. She'd figured out that she ran toward hers. She didn't know what she would say or he would say. Suddenly, she didn't care. The rumor was only a rumor. Probably he needed to know that it wasn't upsetting her. It had, for sure, but between the visit of Letitia to ask advice, with Penny's good friends there to support them both, and this morning's session with Sheila in which her attitude toward learning underwent a huge change, even as Penny watched, she felt up to things again.

So there was a stupid rumor? So it would bother Kenneth if he heard? Even if she felt things for Oscar she didn't understand or know what to do with, life was like that, and she would cope. In the end she always did cope. Life could make you feel underneath everything, but her bounce was returning, and she was feeling a hundred percent better. If she could interest Sheila in subject-verb agreement, who knew what else might be possible?

She glanced at her box. Nothing. She walked on to Oscar's door and stuck her head in. "Are you free?"

He looked up from his computer, startled; then he smiled. "For you, Penny, I am always free."

Uh oh, she thought. My poor heart. How much of this could she take?

She walked in, set her backpack beside the chair closest to the open door, and sat down. "I came to report success number one."

"I could use some good news," he said. "I was glad to see that you held class. You're my only faculty member here this morning, which suggests—more than suggests, which proves—that you're the only responsible faculty member I've got."

"Hardly," Penny said. "I'm probably the only naive one. The whole building's empty. Sammie Hargrave is a very conscientious teacher, but she said the students wouldn't come, so she didn't bother. I had one student, Sheila Green, the one who was arrested at the end of the protest Tuesday. You remember? She was so good on the megaphone?"

He nodded. "See, you hold class, and somebody comes."

"Only Sheila, but that's what I wanted to tell you. She failed the midterm, the grammar test, even though she's quite intelligent."

He had looked quite bleak. Now he was listening intently, his eyes bright and totally focused on her. It was enough to make her run for her life. Keep talking. Say the next sentence and the next, she told herself. You cope well, remember? Then she had a memory suddenly return of how, ten years earlier, she had barely coped with the erotic feelings Kenneth had stirred in her. Now that had been extremely hard. This was minor compared to the feelings Kenneth had awakened. She could cope with this dear man, trying so hard to reform this English Department and, to do that, he had to reform the whole college. She smiled.

"Go on."

"She came to class in her pajamas, if you can believe it, and she looked quite raggedy and beaten down, especially when she heard her midterm grade was a low D."

"Violating Siler's dress code." Oscar smiled for the first time. "But you had the sense to ignore that."

"I persuaded her to stay and work with me on the grammar she'd had trouble with on the test, and she did stay. Oscar, she caught on quickly to everything I went over and was doing it herself and happy about it. I never saw such a turnaround. This is one of the ones who left class early my first day. Remember? She said she had to go to the bathroom, and at nine she walked out. Lashandra, too, and now they're protest leaders, and look what's happening to Sheila's attitude. Do you think it was the protest and being arrested? They kept her in jail twenty-four hours."

Oscar was still smiling as he listened. "No, I think what happened was you. You stopped them in their tracks that first day. You got across the idea that learning was essential to their lives. You may even be why they're protesting. You can't see it, can you? There will be others, Penny. You'll have a big effect here. I hope I'll be able to stay and watch you."

Penny felt overwhelmed by his tribute but puzzled. "Why wouldn't you be here?"

"Siler's actively trying to get rid of me. She does seriously blame me for the protest."

"You?" Penny laughed. "I guess if I did something to set the students off, then she's right, because you hired me."

But Oscar wasn't laughing. "It was one of the best moves I ever made to hire you. No, Siler is desperate. The protest makes her look bad, and she would love to get rid of me. She's looking for any excuse." He turned and stared out the window. Not looking at her, he said, "You heard the rumor?"

"About us?" There it was. Penny felt a little numb. Would she make it even through this? She thought so if he didn't hug her.

"Yes, and I know who started it."

"Blanche Rowan."

"That's what I heard from one of my few friends here besides you. How did you know?"

"She was looking through my classroom door the morning of the protest when we were watching out the window."

"I didn't know that, but she has been trying to get me fired ever since I was hired. Audrey told me one day, when I was in her good graces, that Blanche thinks she should be chair of this department. I also learned that Siler will never give her that job. She wants a black chairman. They wanted me to get rid of Blanche, and I can see why, but she'd never be caught in anything that would compromise her tenure. She's a real bitch, if you'll excuse my saying so. An uptight bitch, too. Not for her Clarkson's seductive ways with students, not that they'll ever fire him for sexual misconduct."

"Siler can't fire you for junk like starting the protest, or …" Penny hesitated, but she needed both to reassure him and let him know where she was standing. "… or that dumb rumor, can she?"

"Of course, she can. Siler's a law unto herself. She controls all the money and all the power. I don't even have a contract."

Penny remembered she had overheard Siler tell Clarkson that, when she ran into them on the elevator, but she asked, "You don't?"

"No. I was promised one when they hired me for a year, and if all went well, a contract for three years, but I have yet to see anything."

"That's terrible."

"It's the least of my worries, Penny. I'm worried they'll come after you before you have a chance to work some more of your magic on these kids."

Penny thought of Ronny and Terence. "There are some I'll never reach."

"Always," he said, "but it's why I'm in education and wanted to teach at an HBCU. There are many who are just waiting for someone to see their potential, believe in them, and watch them take off."

"You've done that, haven't you?" she asked quietly.

She saw tears come into his eyes behind his glasses. He took them off, pulled out a neatly folded handkerchief, wiped his eyes, then his glasses, and replaced them. He stared out the window for a long minute and then looked at her again. "It's what I live for."

~

Penny had three in her Creative Writing seminar, and they were all waiting when she arrived on the dot of ten. Obie, she'd expected. Like Penny, he was working on this pre-break Thursday. Letitia and Lashandra had also come. They seemed embarrassed at being so conscientious but explained that they'd met with President Siler at nine. Sheila had been too wiped out to go with them.

"Sheila came to my eight o'clock," Penny said.

Lashandra immediately apologized. "Oh, Miz Weaver, I'm sorry I missed your class this morning, but at nine we had to meet with the prez."

"No problem," said Penny. "Sheila and I worked on some grammar things she has had trouble with. You did well on the midterm, Lashandra. You didn't miss anything today. Tell me about the meeting with the President. How did that go?"

Obie had arranged their desks in a circle, as usual, and he now moved the extras to one side so the four of them were close together. He shut the door and sat down on Penny's left. Letitia glanced at Obie. "Coach, you okay if we talk about this? Your boys are in our protest, least they were 'til the word came down they'd lose their scholarships."

Obie nodded.

Lashandra said more pointedly, "Coach worried about his job." Then she stared at Obie as if to force his confession.

Obie looked surprised. Penny thought Lashandra had put him on the spot, but it was probably true. She had sensed he was sympathetic to the protest but was trying to do his new job well. He gave Penny one of his looks that said, "You and I understand each other." Finally, he looked back at Lashandra. "It's different for me because I got responsibilities. Students have to choose maybe between losing their scholarship and keeping with the protest. Maybe I'm worried about some of the same things they are, but I have to think how it would look to Coach Cox and the other staff and faculty if I joined a student protest. Did you see Miss Weaver out there Tuesday morning? No, she was holding her class, which she was paid to do. I have work at eight in the morning I'm paid to do, too. So it's different for us."

A very plausible argument, but Penny could tell by the way Lashandra was shaking her dreads that she was skeptical. As soon as he finished speaking, she said again, "Coach worried he'll lose his job," confirming her earlier assessment but in a more accepting tone.

Letitia, sexily dressed, as always, in a low-cut orange sweater and tight jeans with orange trim, said, "Only thing is, Coach Warren, can you respect what we're doing and keep your counsel about what we talk over with Miss Penny? We know she's gonna hold class, no matter nobody else does." She flashed Penny a smile that lit her face from within and expressed both her affection and humor. "But she's with us, no matter. She knows Professor Clarkson did Merilee wrong."

Obie glanced at Penny, then said, "I respect you, Letitia and Lashandra. I'm askin' you not to disrespect me. I do what I can in my circumstances. If you mean, am I gonna go tell Coach Cox everything I hear, no, I ain't. I want things better here at the college like you do, but how I work to make it better might be some different."

Letitia looked at Penny, who smiled at her, then said to Obie, "Respect, Coach, and keeping our confidential talk to your own self is all we ask. We don't disrespect you."

"For wanting to keep your job," Lashandra added, grinning at Obie and shaking her dreads.

The tension eased, and Letitia went on, "President Siler, o' course, won't fire Clarkson. She said he has tenure, but we read the faculty rules, and we know that sexual misconduct leads to firing if it's proved. We got proof. So we told her, but she won't give on that. She said he's a valuable professor, and she doesn't believe he did it. She thinks the student is 'fabricating,' and it's none of our business."

"Did she concede that any of your demands were reasonable?" Penny asked. "Interesting that she scheduled the meeting the very day most students leave the campus."

"She not dumb," said Lashandra. "She want all our problems to just go 'way, but we pressed her on all of it. She say the food nutritious, and they can't afford to spend no more without our fees raised. She say nobody starving. Says we can clean our own dorms, nobody stopping us. That's her way to get us off her back."

"She gave us one," added Letitia. "She said our scholarship and loan money would be available when we get back from spring break, but maybe that was her plan all along. This is March second. We come back the twelfth. She gave herself ten days, and the semester is half over. Hoop-de-doo. No matter a lot of us got no money to go home on."

"No?" asked Penny. "Then where is everybody?"

Lashandra laughed. "Some of 'em's sleeping in they rooms. Sheila and I be going home with 'Titia here, and some got theyselves rides. If they could leave this place, they did. It's some depressing, hafta be here and no money, eat that bad food ten days, nothing happening 'round here."

Thirteen

Sunday, March 11. Sometimes Penny's life felt to her like it was all struggle. One crisis or urgency popped up after another. Then there were what she thought of as halcyon days, the old term for the sea being so calm that the halcyon bird could nest on the waves. The Sunday which was the last day of spring break dawned warm for March and sunny. They'd had a few cold nights but no hard freezes. It had been a rather mild winter, and during their week off Kenneth and Penny had been helping Andy and Jan with their garden. Andy, in turn, had given some time to Kate's apple trees and Penny's peaches, spraying dormant oil on the apples before the blossoms appeared and then an antifungal solution on the peaches when they budded.

The last half of February had been stressful with new jobs for both her and Kenneth, and they hadn't spent much good, relaxed time together for a while. As she woke slowly, a real luxury, she smiled, thinking about their lovemaking the night before.

Dear Kenneth. No, she didn't want anyone else in the bed beside her, his arm flung over her back where she lay on her side. His protectiveness was infuriating at times, but their connection was so solid, so there, no matter what. They had surface misunderstandings, and, of course, they saw Oscar differently. She had been confused by Oscar's need of her and her need to know she was doing well in her new job. Oscar had definitely given her confidence. She still hadn't told Kenneth this turmoil she'd experienced in her feelings about her new boss, but a week away from Oscar and more time with Kenneth had reminded her of the treasure her husband was.

She had almost drifted back to sleep, as she had seen by the bedside alarm clock that it was only seven. They had all day to prepare for the potluck gathering they, Belle, Kate, Jan and Andy were hosting at six that evening. Kenneth's arm began to move over her back, and his fingers reached her left breast.

"You must be awake," she said.

"No, I'm dreaming. There's a beautiful breast in bed with me, and it's doing funny things to me." He began stroking her nipple.

"Now you're doing funny things to me," she said.

"All the better. He lifted himself closer and began kissing the back of her neck after he'd moved her braid to one side.

"We did this only hours ago."

"True, love, and I enjoyed it so much, as did all my parts, and they are asking for more."

She was aflame already in all her parts and whispered, "So are mine."

"Ah, Penny," he said, pulling her around so she was facing him. "What would I do without my Penny?" He put his lips on hers, and she no longer felt any need for words.

At five-thirty that evening, Penny, Kate and Belle were organizing Belle's kitchen for the descent of their guests when Formy announced a car. Penny was washing up a few of the cooking dishes at the sink and saw Rick and Cathy drive in and park their van behind the house. Their boys, Neill and Joe, jumped out of the back. Joe was carrying a basketball that he dribbled, then threw to Neill, who put it through the hoop across the parking lot with ease. Penny watched as little Penny and Kenny, dressed in clean jeans and long-sleeved tee shirts, ran out and clamored to join the game.

Meantime, Belle went to the door and held it for Cathy, who was carrying a big bowl of coleslaw, and Rick, who entered the kitchen with a huge pan of fried chicken. Penny went to welcome them and show them where to put the food. They were setting out all the dishes on the bar counter between Belle's kitchen and living room. They'd left the small dinette table for the children.

Sarah had delivered Seb in the afternoon and agreed that he could spend the night with Leroy. She and Brian had finished her move only the week before and were going to finish unpacking and also take in a movie while Seb was with Leroy. Penny had told Leroy, "It's not all we could wish for, but it's a start."

"I'm taking it a day at a time," Leroy had commented after Seb had settled into his lap, his small arms tight around Leroy's neck. He and Seb would come to the potluck for a little while. "It's our family, Penny, and I like to share him. Family is good for Seb and for me, too." He almost smiled. Penny thought, at least that was one dilemma solved temporarily. She tuned back in to Cathy, who was saying, "We're early, I know, but I can help. Rick, why don't you go play pick up?"

Penny hugged her old friend. "We haven't caught up for a while. It's so good to see you."

Cathy, wearing pressed jeans, a light green turtle neck pullover, and matching hair band over her page boy, said,

"I know. It's terrible. You've been busy at the college, and it seems like I run from one thing to the next between the church and the school PTA. I've been doing right much volunteering in the classroom at the elementary, too. How's the teaching going? Derek says they haven't made any headway on the Provost's murder, and we read about the student protest. What happened to it? Did it fizzle during spring break?"

"Not entirely. By the way, Rick probably set it off. The leaders say Rick inspired them, but President Siler is blaming Oscar."

Rick had been about to go out the back door but now turned back, frowning. "I refuse to take the credit for that protest, Penny. If my talk about the importance of truth and of remembering that we're all in God's hands set off the students, then things were pretty bad long before I got there." He came back into the kitchen and stood by Cathy. "It's not Oscar's fault either, obviously. Did Siler respond at all to the student demands?"

"Not really," said Penny. "The leaders will be here tonight, three of my students, by the way. Letitia Harrelson is Malvina's niece; you probably know her."

"Wasn't she Riverdell's Valedictorian last year?" asked Cathy.

"Yes, and she's an excellent writer, too. Her roommate is Merilee Taylor, the one who slept with her history professor. Then Lashandra Steele, and the other young woman is Sheila Green. They're roommates, and they've been spending the break with Letitia here in Riverdell. I have Sheila in my Pre-Comp class, and Lashandra is in both Pre-Comp and Creative Writing. These are very smart young women. They plan to go to the *News & Observer* and

The Moon, but they want the story to hit after the students come back."

"Tomorrow, right?" asked Rick. "I'd love to talk to them."

"You'll be able to. They were thrilled to learn you were coming, Malvina said. Oh, and Oscar and Maudy are coming, plus Obie and Delois. I wanted our family here to meet my new college friends, and you all are part of our neighborhood family, like Sammie and Derek, who'll be here, too."

"I wish he'd tell us what's up with his case, I mean, the low down scoop," said Cathy.

"He can't, Cathy." Rick was solemn, even scolding, like she should know better. "He has to build a case to take to court, but he told me he was stuck. Leads but no conclusive evidence. I'm surprised he'll leave it for a party. He has been quite preoccupied with it. Sammie told Cathy he works on it all the time. I believe I will go out and play pick up. I see Andy and Kenneth out there now. I haven't seen Andy in ages."

As Rick went out, Jan Style came in. Her dark hair was cut short early this year, maybe because of their warm spring. She was looking more like her mother Belle every day. She'd brought a big salad with fresh garden leaf lettuce, green onions, and red and purple radishes. "I figured I'd bring in the food and see if I can help," she said, smiling. Belle took the salad. "Lovely. Your garden?"

"*Our* garden," Jan insisted, "but, yes, most of it is from our neighborhood garden. Kate, Leroy, Kenneth, Penny and the children have been helping Andy on weekends and in the evenings. All that work is beginning to bear fruit."

Penny walked over to give her a hug. "I haven't seen you nearly enough lately either. Andy explained that you have a long day at your job, leave at five-thirty in the morning now?"

"Yes, and Andy gets the kids off to the bus before he goes to work, but he works right here in Riverdell, of course. As a county agent he has more flexible hours than I do as a natural resources employee, but at least I can go in and then leave early. I get home from Raleigh by three-thirty when their bus comes, but then comes dinner and bedtime rituals, you know. Andy helps a lot, but by bedtime we both fall in bed. I'm out by nine, but hey, I slept in 'til seven this morning. I'm ready for a party, and I've got Neill and Joe lined up to babysit, starting at eight, so we can send all the kids off to our house. A grownup night, and I'm so glad I get to meet your new boss, Penny."

"Me, too. You'll like him and his wife, Jan. Belle, is there anything else you need us for?"

"Nah. You two go sit down and catch up. It's all ready. Kate and I will welcome the guests and organize the dishes as they come in. We haven't had a party in ages, Penny. This is like old times when we had the nuclear wars, the air pollution woes, and the election from hell."

Penny laughed. "Now we have a student protest and a murder, not to mention a professor who trades As for sex. Plenty of problems left to work on, Belle. I'm hoping we'll get into some of them when my students get here, and you and Kate might have ideas for them, at least give them your moral support. The President of the college is treating them shabbily."

Kate walked up. "What's this about a prof that trades As for sex? I haven't run across that one. Sounds like extreme sexual abuse to me." Kate was neat, as always, in her pressed jeans and white, long-sleeved shirt.

"I want the students to consult you, Kate," Penny said, "if you're willing. They're very passionate about how Merilee, who is severely learning disabled, was taken advantage of by her history prof. With all your work for Rape Crisis, you'll be exactly what the doctor ordered. Oh, looks like they've arrived. Malvina was bringing them. Letitia's her niece, and Lashandra and Sheila have been staying with her over the break. Now they'll get to meet the big guns." She smiled at Belle's startled look and noted that Kate had probably not even heard her. She was out the door to welcome the young women.

"Everything's in hand, Jan," Penny said. "Let's sit on the couch. I want to hear more about your job at the Division of Air Quality. It seems only yesterday when you did that research paper on Sampson Pine's air pollution. By the way, Letitia's father works for Sampson Pine, but it has a new name now, I forget."

"Pine Products. We haven't found them out of compliance so far, but we keep on eye on that plant, you may be sure. To think my being at DAQ now all started because of that terrible formaldehyde pollution. I was so young then," said Jan, "and so pregnant and so scared. I couldn't have done it all without you, Penny." She hugged her.

"Of course, you could have and did, but I loved egging you on to make your own choices and be happy. Have you ever regretted having those babies?"

"Never. Andy is so wonderful. We make a good team. You know? If something needs doing and I'm not there or I'm busy, he just does it. We get stretched, but life is good, Penny, and I love having Pen and Ken in first grade. They took to school like ducks to water." Her eyes found her mother welcoming Malvina and her niece and friends. "Mom has come through, too, Penny," she said quietly, "more than I ever imagined. You said way back then that she'd be a doting grandmother. How did you know?"

Penny thought of all the tantrums Belle had thrown since she'd first met her not long after her former husband and Penny's landlord, Jerry Jones, had been murdered in this very house ten years earlier. Belle's rages had diminished amazingly over the years, but she was not one to squelch her anger and occasionally still let it rip. But once Belle had gotten to know Penny, she'd shown her more tender side.

"I knew your mom loved you even when she raged at you. I'm not sure how. Raging was her way of worrying, I guess. Grandchildren are different. You've already gotten your own kids pretty much raised by the time grandkids appear, and they're part of you, after all. What's not to love about a grandchild? I miss Seb a lot when I'm in Wales. He is such a delight. Your twins, too. They're like my first grandchildren."

Malvina had come through into the living room, and Penny stood up to hug her and welcome Letitia, Sheila, and Lashandra. She saw Jan nod to her and slip back toward the dinette. "Have you all had a good spring break?"

"Real good, Miss Penny," said Lashandra. "Letitia's mama done spoiled us rotten. Good home cookin'. It was so good after all that nasty cafeteria food it made me cry."

"I ain't seen no tears," said Sheila, "just you stuffin' your face."

Letitia whispered, "We saw Rev. Clegg out playing basketball. I can't wait to talk to him. We met Miss Kate, the rape crisis lawyer, as we were coming in. She said she'd help us with Merilee's situation. Do you think we should sue the college?"

"Kate would have an opinion," said Penny. "Let me introduce you to Cathy Clegg, Reverend Clegg's wife."

Cathy had been fussing with the various potluck dishes, uncovering them and putting out serving spoons. She now walked up, beaming. She was so easily enthusiastic about their career plans that Penny wanted to hug her.

"A teacher of English and a writer?" she exclaimed to Letitia. "Excellent. I read that you were Riverdell's valedictorian. You're off to a great start, and I'm sure Penny will make you work your tail off and add real serious building blocks to the good foundation you had at Riverdell High. These are your college friends?"

"Yes, ma'am. Lashandra Steele plans on being a TV reporter. Weather, I think."

Lashandra gave Letitia a fearsome look, then smiled at Cathy. She shook her beautifully beaded dreads. "No, ma'am, not weather. Any fool can do weather. I'll be doing world news coverage, the first black woman international TV reporter. Covering Africa probably." She looked at Penny and grinned. "Once I get out of Miss Penny's Comp class, the rest will be easy."

"You right there, girl, no lie. I'm Sheila Green, and Miss Penny the only teacher holding class day before spring break. Then I had to be stupid and go, and Lord, she made me work. 'Bout fried my brain, all them singulars and plurals, fragments and what not." She gave Penny a wicked grin.

"I figured, if she was there and I had her full attention finally, that we could cover the first half of the course. She's a smart young lady." Penny watched Sheila for her reaction.

"Half the course? No joke, Miss Penny?"

"Pretty close. All you have to do is remember and review what I know you understood ten days ago."

"Sheila, what are your life goals?" asked Cathy.

Sheila held Penny's gaze a minute while Penny nodded. Then she seemed unable to stand still. She was dancing in place as she said, "I'll be an actor, ma'am. Maybe on one of them soaps, that's good money, but Broadway would be okay, too. One of those runs that goes on for years."

"I'm impressed," said Cathy. "Now tell me about your protest. Rick and I are eager to learn all we can and support you, too. Like Malvina, we have good friends among the alumni. If we know the whole story, we can spread the word."

Rick walked in, and Penny beckoned him over. Obie and Delois had arrived, and she wanted to speak to them. Malvina had settled on a chair near the girls and would enjoy that discussion. Jan was helping the twins get plates and sit down in the dinette. Neill and Joe had come in to get their food. Belle's house was full. Who was missing? Oscar and Maudy, Sammie and Derek. Seb and Leroy.

Behind Obie and Delois, who were standing near the back door talking with Andy and Belle, she saw Oscar and his wife arrive. They would want to join in the protest discussion. She'd go meet them. She actually felt calm and normal seeing Oscar on her home turf. This would be easier than she had expected.

There was enough food to feed twice the twenty-four people they had gathered. Everyone seemed in good spirits. Here Oscar was valued. He told her with happy eyes how much he'd enjoyed the intense discussion with the three young women about the protest. "There are worse reasons than starting a protest to get fired," he told her. He knew Letitia, but the others he was now proud of, too. "I knew we had better quality students than it seemed," he said as they stood in line to serve themselves. "It's the college experience itself that is doing the damage. We've got to fix it. If Siler can't respond decently, she's got to go."

"Talk to Kate," said Penny. "She's a very sharp lawyer and already sympathetic. She may advise suing the college, and she might be willing to take the case."

Once they had eaten until they couldn't hold any more, including slices of Malvina's old-fashioned pound cake and Sammie's fried apple pies, either or both with ice cream, and the children had gone over to the Styles' to watch TV (later the twins would go to bed, with the Clegg boys to babysit), and Leroy had happily carried off Seb, waving goodbye with energy and even blowing kisses to them, the rest found chairs or floor space in Belle's and Kate's living room, and talk turned to the protest again.

By that time they were all caught up on the details, and the activists present wanted to "solve this thing once and for all," as Belle put it. Even Derek was interested and attentive. Sammie had told Penny that she had to "light a fire under his butt" to get him to come. Her winning argument had been, "How you gonna know who killed the Provost if you don't know the inside happenings at the college? Believe me, Penny and Oscar and the three freshmen who set off the protest are right in there."

Penny was very glad he'd left his case for a few hours and involved himself in learning about the college's problems as seen by the students and the faculty present, although she hardly felt the way Sammie painted her as inside.

"It's so obvious," said Kate. "The college needs to fire that history prof. They're leaving themselves wide open to a suit if they don't. It might be possible to sue over the dirty dorms and bad food, especially if a Health Department inspection of the kitchen turned up problems." Her look was stern, but this rallying cry to the students' cause made them all beam. Lashandra was shaking her dreads to invisible music, and then she got up and danced around, humming, "We shall overcome."

Sheila said, "Sit down, 'Shandra. This be serious. Miss Kate a real lawyer. We gonna nail old Siler now."

"But don't legal cases cost money?" asked Letitia.

"*Pro bono*," said Kate. When Letitia looked blank, she added, "It means no fee, but I think we should go after Clarkson first and his abuse of Merilee. Do you think she and her parents would be willing to sue the college and Siler if I gave my time?"

Penny was thinking that that might be too much for Merilee, expose her vulnerability too painfully, when Letitia spoke up. "I don't know, Miss Kate. Merilee's pretty shy. She let us include her situation in the protest, but a legal suit might be too hard on her. She's not very savvy. That's why the prof found it so easy to take advantage of her. I'd worry about her if it went that big."

Lashandra said, "She been with us so far, 'Titia. We goin' to the newspapers tomorrow. So what's that gonna do? Her story might go out on the wire and get picked up by papers in other places. Those TV stations might go for it, too. I think we need to ask her. I think she and Ronny and them are coming back tonight. Let's ask her."

Kate nodded. "I agree. Her story is already out there. The TV news people could happen on it anytime. Do you have a way of contacting her parents?"

Letitia said, "Let me talk to her first when she gets back. Dad will carry us back to the college after Miss Penny's potluck."

"If Merilee and her parents don't want to instigate the suit," said Kate, "there must be other young women. Men like Clarkson, especially by his age--Penny, didn't you say he was in his sixties?--often are quite repetitive with this kind of behavior."

Malvina protested. "Hey, y'all, I'm in my sixties. Don't go knocking no sixties. These are fine years. I ain't had so much fun since I retired and went full time as an activist."

Penny jumped in. "There's a world, and I mean a world, of difference between you and Clarkson, Malvina. I'm sixty-four, and life is good. Teaching these freshmen,"and here she looked happily at the three of them in front of Malvina and Oscar on the floor, hugging their knees and hanging onto her words, "had its challenges, but now it's fun. They're starting to work. I love to make people work." The girls laughed with her, and Sheila groaned. Oscar gave Penny a long, searching look that seemed to say, "You're such a treasure."

Penny hoped Kenneth, who was across the room by Derek, didn't see it. As she thought that, she realized that as much as she loved Kenneth, she loved Oscar, too, for just such spontaneous and complete recognition of who she was and what she was like. She certainly didn't have any answers, but there it was. She had no choice but to feel what she felt. Then she saw Maudy looking at her. If Kenneth had missed Oscar's look, Maudy hadn't.

"Miss Kate, I'm not sure a suit is the way to go, especially not with Merilee," Maudy said. "If she were my daughter, I wouldn't want her out there exposed like that. It's well and good to talk suing the college, but the college has no money to pay damages or hire its own lawyers. They'll turn on Oscar and Penny, maybe Sammie and Obie, too, and fire you all. They're holding the axe over Oscar's head now. They'll expel these three freshmen— well, four, Merilee, too—and sweep everything under the table. There must be better, more long-term solutions, less confrontational."

Penny watched Belle, who was sitting beside Kate, come to the boiling point and fidget. Then her face turned red, and she started tapping her foot, glancing at Kate. Finally she blew. "What you've got, Maudy, is a diseased administration. From what you've all said, the college has been going down the tubes for several years, and this Clarkson has tenure, and they're afraid to fire him. The black President is afraid to fire the horny old white man, so she doesn't interrupt his sick game with freshman girls, disabled girls? Geez. Somebody has to blow the whistle. That's not a college. It's a whore house."

Uh oh, thought Penny. This will do it. She caught Jan's eye and smiled. Oscar, however, also disagreed with Maudy. He looked right at his wife and said, "Belle, you're right. It's not a college. The Provost herself told me the day before she died that they couldn't fire Clarkson for sexual misconduct, or they'd have to fire half the faculty."

Maudy's face went blank, which very effectively hid her feelings.

"Now wait, Mr. Oscar," said Obie. He glanced at Belle. "We have some good things happening at the college, too. Problems, yes, but it's not all bad. My football boys are a little rowdy, and most of them hate to study, but between me and Miss Penny, they're coming around. Miss Sammie and Mr. Oscar himself, I know, are strict. There are ways to work on this without taking no case to court."

Malvina had watched everyone's faces with her usual keen interest. "I agree that a suit might do more harm than good, but remember, the protest itself is a sign of health. St. Francis ain't dead yet. These young people, and I include Penny and you, too, Oscar, and Obie and Sammie, you're going to win this thing by being who you are and letting the wider world know. Those newspaper stories are going to bring that Board of Trustees to their knees, and they'll settle Christine Siler's feathers better than any of us can do."

Fourteen

Tuesday, March 13. "I can't say I'm sorry," said Sammie as she zoomed past a white, extra-long, two-ton truck in morning traffic headed into Raleigh.

"No one deserves to be murdered," said Penny, unconsciously pressing her foot to the floor as Sammie swerved back into the lane she needed for merging onto the 440 beltway around Raleigh.

"You too kind, girl. What a bastard old Clarkson was. Only bad part is that his murderer will have to pay. Let's hope it wasn't a student."

Clarkson's dead body had been found in his History Department office Monday morning the day before, when classes resumed. Sammie had been there when he didn't show up for his ten o'clock class Black History class. When Sammie called, his wife said he'd been out all night, and they found his office door locked with the light on inside. When they got Rosa to use her master key to unlock his office, they found him in his chair, his pants down. He'd been beaten about the face and chest and strangled with a doo-rag.

Sammie had shut the door and told Rosa to stay and guard it while she went to her office to inform the police. Then she'd asked Oscar to come down and help them keep students and others away. Oscar summoned the President from her home and Rob Grubb from his office via their secretaries, and he stayed right with Sammie until the Raleigh police arrived. Sammie had called Derek, too.

Monday evening she'd called Penny and caught her up. "Your boss should be clear now. It happened early Sunday evening, not after ten, and Oscar was with us at the potluck. Derek's really embarrassed that he still has him under a bond. Not much longer, I think. They arrested Terence in the afternoon. They already had his DNA from before the break, when Derek was interviewing students, and they are trying to match his DNA to some hairs on the doo-rag. For now the charge is possession of drugs. He had reefers on him, but Derek says the doo-rag is exactly like the one he was wearing when they talked before the break."

"And Merilee? Ronny? What do they know? They rode up with Terence. Did they also ride back with him? They've all been hanging around together."

"That's the curious part," Sammie had said. "Merilee and Ronny say they didn't get back to campus until early Monday morning. They did ride back from Camden with Terence."

Now, as Sammie pulled in and parked on College Avenue, Penny asked, "Has anyone talked to Merilee and Ronny besides the police?"

"Not as far as I know. Merilee was waiting in the hall for a class when it happened, and I saw the police take her into an empty classroom to talk to her. She was crying, but they wouldn't let me go in with her. I told Derek they should all go easy with her. He said he didn't have much power with this case yet. Raleigh isn't sure there's any connection between the two cases. Derek is sure there is. If it turns out he's right, he'll have more say-so. Maybe you can talk to Merilee. You have her in class this morning, don't you?"

"Yes. I'll see if I can catch her after class. I wonder if they called her mother."

"God knows," said Sammie. "Come on, girl, we got to get our own selves to class. Yesterday hardly any students came to class. Scary for them, I guess, a prof being killed, even if he deserved it. What was he up to anyway with his pants around his ankles?"

As it happened, neither Merilee nor Ronny was in Penny's eight o'clock class. Half the class was absent. Lashandra and Sheila came. Penny picked up how restive they were, whispering to each other and looking away when she glanced at them. She had planned to introduce compound and complex sentences, but instead, she invited them to tell her what they knew or thought about the murder.

"We didn't want him dead," Lashandra volunteered, "just gone. He was a nasty man. If he'd been fired when we asked the Prez to fire him, he'd probably be alive."

There were murmurs of agreement. "Anyone else?" Penny sensed their worry. It was important, she knew, to get young people to talk about something this traumatic. They brought in therapists to talk with high school students when a fellow student was killed in a car accident. These young people weren't much older, and many were like children emotionally. She waited. She caught Sheila's eye and nodded to encourage her to speak up.

"Miss Penny, we scared. Maybe the police blame us on account of our protest."

Penny hadn't thought of that. "I don't think they'd blame you for protesting Professor Clarkson's sexual misconduct," she said.

Larry, one of the football players, raised his hand. "Police don't listen to us, Miz Weaver. I got arrested one time. I ain't done nothin'. I was driving back from a concert with my girlfriend, and they pull me over, make me get out my car and bend over. I ain't had no gun or nothin, and they looked all over my car. There was nothin', no drugs, nothin', but they carried me to jail. Turned out some guy robbed a store, and he was black and wearing a red shirt. I was wearing a red shirt. I was in that jail two days before my family could get me out. They ain't seen us as people, Miz Weaver. We just black and must be doin' somethin' wrong."

The others nodded and murmured, "Sure do." "That how it go down."

Sheila said, "It ain't right, Miss Penny, but it do happen. My cousin one time was driving in a nice white neighborhood, going to a party at a friend's house. Police stopped him, said he ran a stop sign and went over the speed limit, and he ain't. But they give him a ticket anyway. Wasn't nothin' he could do."

Penny began to understand their fear now. What to say? How could she reassure them? "Both those things that happened, Sheila and Larry, were very wrong. Police do make mistakes. They arrested Terence, I understand. Do you think that was a mistake?"

"Yes, ma'am," said Larry. "He in my dorm. He a very cool dude. He play a mean game. He our wide receiver. Ronny say they got back yesterday morning, not no

Sunday night. Ronny say they found a reefer on Terence, so they carried him to jail."

"Does anyone know if he has a lawyer?"

"No, ma'am," said Larry. "He ain't rich. He got his car, but he got babies back in Camden, got to send his wife most his money, he tol' me."

"I know a lawyer who might help him," Penny said. "I'll find out if he needs one. If anyone else has information, come see me in the Writing Center or call me at home. If you see them, please tell Merilee and Ronny to come to class. We still have work to do, and it will keep your minds from worrying so much. Now what do you think a compound sentence would be?"

Once her students had left the room, Penny packed up and walked straight to Oscar's office. Oscar welcomed her, as he always did. He looked worried, though. "Did you have students?" he asked.

"Yes, but about half were absent, including Merilee and Ronny. I'm worried about Merilee. Have we a way of getting in touch with her? She rode back with Terence. I'd like to make sure she's okay."

"Let me call the Dean of Women and see if they can find her. You want them to bring her here?"

"I don't want to scare her, Oscar. She's probably already scared. I would like to talk to her if she'd come on her own. I wouldn't force her to come. Can you ask them to get a message to her to come and see me in my office hours?"

Sammie poked her head around the door. "Can I interrupt?"

"Of course, Sammie. Come in, but I'm going to shut my door." Oscar moved to it. "Blanche is in her office about now. I don't want any more rumors floating around." He smiled at Sammie and gestured her to a chair. She sat down by Penny.

"The students are scared shitless," she said. "Yours, Penny?"

"Yes," said Penny. "They're afraid they'll be blamed for Clarkson's murder because of the protest. They told me stories of the police arresting the wrong people. They don't think Terence killed him. He apparently needs a lawyer. I'm thinking Kate would help him."

"I wish Derek could be more involved," said Sammie.

"He's still not?" Penny was surprised. "Even I can see a connection between the murders, even if it's only being in the same college. Surely they'd want to know what Derek knows and Kenneth, too."

"Oh, they asked Derek for his file, but they're holding him off. He says with Terence's doo-rag maybe going to provide a DNA match, they won't be doing much investigating. They think they've already solved it."

"Dead white man. Black kid whose DNA is on the murder weapon? Not to mention that Terence is from a city where murder is common. He sells drugs there and here. It would be a rare lawyer who could do much to save him," said Oscar.

Penny looked at Sammie, who nodded, and then at Oscar. "Kate could do it. She got Rick off when corrupt Shagbark politicians had him sitting in jail. In fact, she has been his lawyer several times."

Sammie jumped up. "You got her work number? Let's call her."

Oscar walked to his desk and handed Sammie the phone. Penny dug into her backpack for her emergency numbers and handed her list to Sammie.

Oscar came over to Penny and said quietly, "Defending Rick, a minister and respected leader, is one thing. Saving this Camden drug dealer is another. Even if Terence didn't kill Clarkson, he'll be seen as guilty."

Penny saw the despair in his face, but what to say?

Someone knocked. Oscar opened his door a crack and then wider. "Come on in, Derek. We're working on getting Terence a lawyer."

Derek stepped in, and Oscar closed and locked the door. Sammie was saying, "You can, Kate? That's great. I'm not sure where they have him." She looked up and saw Derek. "Oh, good. Derek's here. He'll know. Derek, where are they holding Terence?"

"Downtown Raleigh station."

Sammie relayed the information, thanked Kate and hung up.

Derek turned to Oscar. "I brought the paperwork to release you from the bond. Sorry about that, Oscar. I didn't know you or this college very well when I did that."

Penny knew Derek hated to admit he'd made a mistake, but he was too honest not to when it was crystal clear. But how would Oscar take it?

"We've got bigger problems," Oscar said. "I think they'll frame Terence for the murder. They've already got him on a drug charge, and they'll add the murder to it. He could have killed Clarkson." He smiled. "I was angry enough to do it, but Terence needs a fair chance."

"I totally agree, Oscar, and they won't let me touch it. They think it's all sewed up. I don't know if you knew this,

Oscar, and I hate like hell to admit it, but Penny here and my wife have helped me more than I usually tell people in some very tough cases. I came partly to ask them to help me with this one. So we need to find out what really happened. I'm not officially part of this new investigation, but I'm still working on the Provost's murder, and I'm sure there's a connection somewhere."

~

After her seminar Penny walked over to the student union. She needed some information from the bookstore as to how many texts had been sold for her composition class. By emailing the numbers to the publisher, she could receive some supplementary reading material free. She had yet to hear from Merilee. Maybe she would call her mother and say she just wanted to help her, if she could.

The bookstore manager turned out to be in her closet-sized office near the front of the store. The upper half of the door was folded down, so she said to the woman at the only desk, who was working on some papers, "Excuse me. Could I speak to the manager?"

"I'm the manager, Adele Davis." She wasn't smiling to see a white lady instructor at her window.

"Hi, I'm Penny Weaver, teaching English 21 now. Could you tell me how many of the English 21 textbooks have been sold so far this semester?"

Adele studied her, not apparently liking what she saw. "If I may ask, why would you need to know that?"

"If I send in the number of books sold, I can receive some free reading material from the publisher for my students. They need to be reading more to write better." Penny smiled.

Adele glanced at Penny. "I'm sorry, I can't release that information." Then she looked back down at her papers as though, as far as she was concerned, that was the end of their conversation. Now all Penny had to do was go away, but Penny had never given up that easily.

"Could you please explain to me why you can't tell me the number of books sold?" Penny was thinking, this is ridiculous. What could possibly be the problem here? But she held onto her patience. She hadn't before at this campus been so aware of being seen as a pain and a nuisance, merely because she was white.

"I'm not allowed to release those numbers," Adele said without looking up.

Penny hesitated, but she could be stubborn, too. "I don't understand. It seems easy enough to do. After all, it benefits the students."

At that moment a man appeared in the other doorway to Adele's closet office. "Sorry to interrupt you, Adele, but can we go over the pricing of the new inventory now?"

He was very tall, probably in his sixties, as his brown curly hair had some grey streaks in it. Where had she seen this stout man with the light skin and freckles? Ah, it was Robert Grubb, the Finance Officer and new Provost, Oscar's chief nemesis, not counting the President. He had introduced Rick at the convocation. Aha. So he was Adele's boss. Maybe he could help get her the numbers.

"I'm free," said Adele. "She," she implied Penny but without indicating that by look or gesture, "wants to know the number of texts we sold for English 21, but I told her I couldn't release that information without your permission, of course."

"Quite right, Adele. Miss …?"

"Penny Weaver."

"Miss Weaver, I'm the Finance Officer, Robert Grubb. That information is confidential." He stepped closer to the window, as if daring her to contest his judgment. He was wearing another beautifully tailored suit and a silk vest, in dark blue this time with a light blue shirt and handkerchief in his upper jacket pocket. His shoes were polished to a high shine, and everything about him declared him elegantly turned out and very prosperous.

Penny wasn't easily intimidated. "I want to take advantage of a publisher's offer of free books for my Pre-Comp students. All I need are these sales numbers. I have twenty-five students, and most now have texts. About twenty, I think. Couldn't you let me have your verification of that?"

"No, sorry," he said, turning so that his back was to her. Then he said to Adele, "Could you come check something for me? I have a question about the American History text." She got up. By now, being totally ignored by them both, Penny was angry. She blurted out. "I'll need to speak to my chairman about this then."

Only after they were almost out of the room did Grubb turn back. "Farrell?" he asked, incredulous.

"Yes," she said.

He shrugged and kept walking.

When Penny got back to his office, Oscar hit the roof. "She what?"

Penny repeated the conversation with Adele. Oscar walked to his desk, consulted a campus directory, picked up the phone, and dialed. "Dr. Grubb, please."

Apparently he wasn't able to talk to him. He slammed down the phone and grabbed his suit coat off the coat tree, which rocked but did not fall over. "I'll get to him," he said, "if I have to break down the door."

Penny picked up her backpack. "Don't do anything rash," she said, smiling. "I'll be in the library, third floor, under the Zora Neale Hurston poster."

He nodded, unsmiling, and strode off, his steps quick and his whole air one of brooking no nonsense. Penny didn't envy Rob Grubb.

~

When Sammie dropped Penny at home a little before four, she saw Andy working in the orchard, wearing his backpack sprayer. She hadn't been paying attention. Her peaches were blooming, and there were buds coming along behind them on Kate's apple trees. The peach flowers were a pale pink and too early. March had scarcely begun, and it was warm today, but the average last frost date was the end of March. She dropped her backpack on the steps leading up their apartment and walked to the orchard gate, letting herself in.

"Hi, Andy. You're already spraying?"

"Yes, it's the lime sulphur. It helps to do it during the blossom phase, more effective than waiting for the fruit to show. Stay back."

"Can the peaches get through to April? I'm worried after all this warm weather that we'll still have a late freeze or even a normal freeze this time of year."

"I'm worried, too, Penny." Andy shifted his ladder and climbed to spray the highest branches. Penny's peach trees had grown amazingly in five years. With Andy to help her, they'd had several good crops relatively free of fungus and the plum curculio, which liked to lay its egg so its worm would dine on peach flesh as the fruit ripened. Once the harvest came in of her Georgia Belle and Carolina Belle peaches in mid- to late July, she gave them away to neighbors and friends, made peach jam, and was still preserving peaches well into August. But a freeze?

"It's always a risk in North Carolina with apples and other fruit, but especially peaches. It's why Georgia and South Carolina have more peach growers than we do. These trees have decided spring is here. No way to stop them now."

"I hope they'll make it," she said. "Now I'd better get to work. Thanks for spraying. You heard about the second murder at the college?"

"Yes, on the news. Be careful, Penny."

"I will. I'm not important enough to be in danger. A Provost and the Chairman of the History Department. It's worrisome though. See you later."

She had changed into her jeans and had a snack of homemade yoghurt and some raw carrots when Formy crowed. She looked out. Malvina and Letitia were getting out of her car. Penny went to the screen door and held it open for them. "What's up, ladies?"

"Are we interrupting anything?"

"No. I'm having a break before I start reading student papers. Come on in. What can I do for you?"

Malvina looked grim, and Letitia, somber.

Penny realized her mood was too cheerful for them. She gestured to the couch. "Can I get you anything to drink? Juice? Tea? Water?"

"You have any of that peppermint tea you make?" asked Malvina as she settled on one end of the couch.

"It only takes a minute. Coming right up." Penny turned on the kettle. "You, Letitia? What can I get you?" She smiled at her, hoping to ease her solemn look.

"Tea is good for me, too, Miss Penny. We're so worried. You know we're going to the press with our protest demands, but it seems strange now with Dr. Clarkson dead. Firing him was one of our main demands. Lashandra thinks that if we keep on protesting, they'll arrest more students, blame us for his death."

Penny turned from the teakettle and looked at Malvina. She wasn't ready to talk yet. Here goes, thought Penny. If I'm out of line, I'm sure Malvina will tell me. "It complicates things," she said, "and it scares the students."

Letitia nodded vigorously.

"The issues are all still there, right?"

"Yes, ma'am. Of course, we can't ask Clarkson to resign." She smiled for the first time.

"No, but from what Oscar learned, Clarkson wasn't the only professor seducing students, which is forbidden by the St. Francis rules for faculty and staff."

"Yes, ma'am."

"Have you heard any stories or rumors about other professors doing that?"

"Not really. A few of the older girls didn't seem shocked like we were when Merilee told us. One of them said, 'You babies are in the real world now.' I think she meant it had happened before, but I'm scared to push those seniors about it with this murder and all."

"Understandable, but what could you do, say, in your press release?"

"We could demand that any staff who violate the sexual misconduct rules be fired, that the college enforce its own rules."

"Of course you could," said Penny.

Letitia smiled broadly. "Miss Penny, would you be willing to look over the press release after I fix the part about Clarkson?"

"Of course."

"We'd like to call *The Moon* and see if they could meet us here in Riverdell instead of at school. We want this to be anonymous, you know?"

"I could call Lila Jones, who covers Shagbark for *The Moon* and invite her for supper. She has helped us before. Of course, you'd have to stay, too."

"Oh, would you, Miss Penny?"

"Of course. Let's see what you've got in your release so far."

Then Malvina smiled.

Fifteen

Thursday, March 15. "It's all over now," Oscar announced as he walked into Penny's classroom and locked the door behind him.

It was 7:20 a.m. on Thursday, and Penny had hoped to have a few minutes of peace and quiet to think; but one look at Oscar on the edge of weeping, and she turned over her diary pages and said, "What's happened now?"

"This." He produced yesterday's *Moon*. Front page headlines: Second Murder Could Have Been Prevented. The girls' plan to be anonymous wasn't working that well. The headline sounded just like Lashandra.

Sammie had read it to her over the phone the afternoon before. Who else but the protest leaders would know the details and leak them?

"I knew about it," she said to Oscar. "Aren't you glad the word is out more widely about the student protest? It should make the President look really bad."

He slapped the paper down on the student desk in front of her and sat down. He was already calmer. He needed to talk about it. Her diary could wait. True, it had been waiting a lot lately. "It does make the President look bad and Clarkson, White and Grubb. It makes the whole college look corrupt and mismanaged. Siler and Grubb are furious. They've been down to *The Moon* headquarters to talk to the publisher. They're threatening to sue. They haven't a leg to stand on. Everything that was leaked is true."

"Of course, it's true. I was there when it was leaked," said Penny, "but I don't understand why you're upset. Isn't this what you wanted? The truth is out now. Remember what Rick said? 'The truth will set you free'?"

She probably shouldn't have added that, but he deserved it. He had wanted everything to change. Rick had called him a catalyst, and she wondered now for the first time if he had any idea what that meant. It didn't mean going on a picnic. It meant that when you acted in such a way or spoke the truth that threatened the status quo, everything began to change. At least that had been her experience. She had been a catalyst over and over. It set off a dark night of the soul for the catalyst person, but it was often the only way to shine light on the situation. No more murky corners or subtle, or not-so-subtle, blackmail.

He bristled. Then he said with heavy sarcasm. "Oh, I'll be free, all right. They're going to fire me."

"Why?"

"They keep saying I'm to blame for the protest. If I hadn't encouraged the students, it never would have happened. They think I leaked the story to the press."

"But you didn't, and I didn't either."

"You were there, you said?"

"Yes, it happened in my apartment. I guess you could say I aided and abetted the leak. Anyway, my students are the protest leaders. I'm the one who looked over their press release and invited *The Moon* reporter, a friend of mine, over for supper. It never occurred to me that you wouldn't want the word to get out. You've been telling me everything that's wrong here from the day I began teaching."

"In confidence," he snapped.

"Yes. Oscar, I haven't betrayed your confidence." Now she felt sad. He seemed so caught up in maybe getting fired. He wanted everything to change, but he didn't want to take the consequences of its changing? He didn't understand such a basic thing as that, when you picked up a weapon, your opponent picked up one, too?

He looked at her steadily, then dropped his eyes. "I'm sorry. You're right. I wanted the whole superstructure to topple, but I didn't want to go with it. I'm not angry at you."

"Or the students? Our amazing, intelligent, brave students trying to make their college better? They understand the risks they're taking."

He shook his head. "It's not you. It's not the students. I'm proud of them."

Penny was thinking, this sounds better, more like the Oscar I know.

Then he said, "It's my wife Maudy. She's scared. She's afraid of what will happen to me, to us, if I lose this job and can't get another one. If they do fire me, they'll be after me as long as I'm in a college or university. I'll be an outcast. I'll be ruined."

"Join the club," said Penny. "Rick and I, Sammie, these brave freshmen, we're already outcasts. Rick has been jailed, I lose track of how many times. I've had people full of vicious hate after me. Sammie has more than once engaged with a killer, used karate to bring him down. Little Sammie, and her academic career is all ahead of her, but when she read me that story," Penny gestured to the newspaper on his desk chair, "Sammie was jubilant.

"So they can fire you, Oscar? They can fire me and Sammie. But the word is out now, and every move they make to get rid of the speakers of truth makes them look worse and worse."

He was listening with a new light in his eyes.

"It's like the tar baby," she went on, "the tar baby that did in Brer Rabbit. They're fighting with a tar baby, and every time they lash out, they get more stuck. The light of truth is shining on them now, and they can't escape. You'll be all right."

Then he did stand up, wipe his eyes and hug her. This time she hugged him back, for the moment not considering what that implied for him or for her. Through the window in her door she saw Lashandra mouthing, "Unlock the door."

"My students are here," she said. "It must be nearly eight." A glance at her watch told her it was five minutes of.

"Teach, Penny. Teach them like you teach me," he said and walked fast to the door and out it. Lashandra danced in, holding the same newspaper as the one he'd left on the student desk. "We did it, Miss Penny. Front page."

Derek and Oscar hunted Penny up at the end of her seminar and went with her to the Writing Center. She had missed her office hours several times and had sent word to Merilee to meet her there, so she was determined to be there herself. Oscar looked less ragged and more confident. "The students in both my classes were so happy," she told them when they had settled around the table at the back of the room. "Everyone was there but

Merilee, Ronny and, of course, Terence. The newspaper story makes them feel acknowledged, important, justified. They literally swell with pride. On Tuesday they were so scared. It's amazing."

Oscar beamed at her as if to say it was not surprising to him, but Derek looked worried.

"Derek, what's the news? Are they still keeping you off the case?"

"Yes. I did learn something interesting. I shouldn't tell you." He paused. Penny had rarely known him to give away part of his investigation except to Kenneth, who was also a detective. Then Kenneth always told her, which Derek hated. But this was new, his volunteering information to her and even to Oscar. She waited.

"We found some fingerprints on whiskey glasses at Audrey White's house from the night she was killed. Hers, but the other glass didn't have her husband's prints. When they fingerprinted the deceased Clarkson, they got a match. Clarkson must have been there that night."

Penny said, "Sammie had heard a rumor they were having an affair, right? She told you, right?"

He nodded. "It's so hard when your wife is right and you're wrong."

"Don't say that," said Oscar. "Penny has convinced me to do what's right, come hell or high water, with my wife." He looked at her and smiled.

"Different problem," she said. "Anyway, that's very interesting, Derek. Do you think he killed her?"

"I don't know what to think," said Derek. "You'd think the Raleigh detectives would want me working with them, wouldn't you? But not so far, not even when there's this new connection between the White and Clarkson murders, and that's not the worst. Everything I hear sounds bad for Terence."

"They don't want to look further," said Oscar. "They've got a black drug dealer suspect to crucify, maybe for both murders."

"He may have been at Audrey White's, too. I really am trusting you guys. We think Terence was supplying her cocaine. She had apparently taken some, and there was a little of it on her bedside table. It was folded into a lined notebook page torn from the kind of composition book that the college bookstore here sells."

"Good God," said Oscar. "They'll pin Audrey's murder on him, too, for sure."

"Maybe not. The evidence isn't there to connect him to her killing, no fingerprints that match his, but we have our suspicions. I was able to see him yesterday about Audrey's case. He's very scared, and he tells me they're beating him where bruises don't show unless you strip. He also claims he lost his doo-rag, that he didn't kill her. On that I'm not sure what to believe. Kate's his lawyer, but I don't know if she can do anything. It's his word against theirs. I'm tempted to believe him though."

Oscar shook his head. "Damn, damn, damn. Penny, it's like I told you weeks ago. This was Terence's last chance, and there it goes." His face was bleak.

"Kate's good," said Penny. "Call her, Derek. See what she says. I heard they found reefers on him. Did they find cocaine, too?"

"No, only a few reefers. It's simple possession. We know he sells, but so far we can't prove it. I called the Camden police. They know him well. They have never caught him selling either, but his house of cards is falling down around his ears now."

Penny thought of his three little children. Oscar got up suddenly and walked away fast. She was sure he was seeing the desperate faces in that prison van.

The temperature began dropping at noon. Penny noticed it as she crossed the street between Booher Hall and the library. By three, when she and Sammie walked to her car, it was bone-chillingly cold. Penny tried to be prepared for weather changes, which were frequent in central North Carolina. She had worn her raincoat with the wool lining and a hood that morning and was glad for its warmth. Sammie had relied on her suit jacket and was shivering. She turned the car heater on high.

By the time Sammie dropped her off, it was even colder. According to the thermometer outside their apartment, it was already down to thirty-six degrees. She dropped her things in the living room and walked back down. She'd seen Andy pruning in the orchard. He had on a sweatshirt and knitted hat.

"Is it going to freeze, Andy?"

He stepped down off the ladder. "It could, Penny. They've got frost warnings out." The peach trees were so beautiful, and now the pink apple buds were opening their white blossoms.

"Is there anything we can do?"

"Not really. We can hope it's not a hard freeze down in the twenties. That would pretty well kill this year's peach and apple crop and my Scuppernong grapes, too." He gestured to the orchard fence, where his grape vines ran along it on both the garden and the orchard side. Pale green leaves had everywhere made their appearance, but a month too early.

"That's so frustrating," she said. "I've often thought that what will eventually do away with the human race is weather--too hot, too cold, too wet, too dry."

"Could be." He'd moved to the Scuppernong and was clipping some of the long runners. "Farming is so high risk, so dependent on rain, sun, no freezes at the wrong time. It's a wonder farmers do as well as they do. Then we've been plagued by drought, too, in recent years.

"Leroy's chickens are flourishing. He must be happy with his hens. They always lay best in the spring, but he says since January, this group of twelve hens is laying nearly twelve eggs a day, and that's toward the end of their first laying season. They're nearly a year old now. That's quite good."

Leroy must have heard them talking. He ducked out of the hen house with his egg basket and walked over.

"Your turn, Penny. Thirteen today."

"Wow, Leroy, thanks. Enough for two more pans of custard. Your eggs are such a treat, but it wasn't my turn for eggs yet, was it?"

"I don't need any right now," Leroy said. "Seb can't come any more."

Penny had been watching the white hens pecking and fluttering here and there in their run. She looked into Leroy's eyes. They looked dull. "Sarah," she started.

"She says that man she's with doesn't want Seb to visit me."

Penny nodded, watching Leroy. She wished she had control over Sarah, over the weather, over what was happening to Merilee and Terence. But she didn't.

Leroy shrugged. "My fault. I should have married her."

Andy had come over to stand with them.

"As I remember," he said, "Sarah didn't want to be married."

"Now she does," said Penny, "to Brian, but I wish she wouldn't cut out Leroy. He's good for Seb."

"I love him is all," said Leroy. "That's not good enough for Sarah." He gave Penny the basket of eggs. "See ya later." He walked off quickly across Andy and Jan's back yard to his basement apartment.

"Isn't there anything he can do? He's Seb's father."

Penny felt so sad at first she couldn't answer. "I suggested he talk to Kate. I think he's going to wait Sarah out. I can't seem to get through to her. She's suddenly determined to build her nuclear family."

"Maybe Jan can help?"

"Maybe," said Penny. "Sarah is pretty resistant to my advice."

"Surely, she's not keeping Seb away from you?"

"No. She wants me to babysit more. Rather tricky all around since Leroy lives so close by. She might be more receptive to Jan."

Andy walked closer and hugged her. "I'll never forget how you helped us so much, Penny, when Jan and I were young and foolish."

She had tears in her eyes after that hug. "Everything is hard today," she said, "the frost, then these students, and now little Seb."

Then she looked down at the beautiful brown eggs–skin tones of various shades from light pink to deep brown. "I'll make custard for us all."

"Farmers have to do that all the time," Andy said, "swing with the punches, go with the crops they have, not waste time worrying when they can't do anything."

Sixteen

Sunday, March 18. That Sunday Penny and Kenneth declared a day off to be together, relax and catch up their home chores. In such a small apartment you couldn't be a packrat, which was Penny's natural inclination. She let Kenneth play the role of going through cupboards and closets, even the refrigerator, making sure they needed what Penny was saving, and then he would borrow Andy's pickup truck and make a run to the recycle center, dropping off anything useful to others in the sheltered area called the Swap Shop. If Penny went with him, she would find dishes or pans or a shirt that she wanted to bring home, so she agreed it was better for her not to go.

Andy and the twins often went along, and they took the whole neighborhood's trash and recyclables. The twins loved throwing the green, brown and clear glass bottles into those bins to hear them smash as they hit the other glass in the big dumpsters. They sometimes found a used toy that Andy let them bring home.

It was another warm, sunny day. The Thursday night before it had hovered a little above freezing, but the grapes, apple and peach trees were safe. Only a few weeks to go before the danger of a late frost would have passed. If they could only get to Easter, which was April fifteenth this year. There was rarely a frost that late, and North Carolina farmers traditionally planted their summer gardens on Easter Monday.

The trash run crew had gotten off at five, and Penny was sautéing chopped onions, garlic and green peppers from the freezer for refried pinto beans when the phone rang.

"Miz Weaver? It's Irene Taylor, Merilee's mother. I'm calling about Merilee's midterm grades."

Penny turned off the fire under the vegetables and sat down on the couch, her feet on the coffee table, less cluttered than it had been with newspapers and miscellaneous mail. Kenneth had left only *The Moon*'s Sunday edition and a stack of bills he was going to pay when he got back from the trash run.

"Yes, Irene. How did she do overall?"

"Not as good as last semester. They've put her on academic probation."

Penny was not surprised. Merilee had a very low F in her Pre-Comp English class.

"I don't understand how she could get Fs in all her classes, Miz Weaver. Math, I understand. She has a hard time with math. I never liked math either."

Penny wondered if Derek or the Raleigh cops had talked to Irene about when Terence, Ronny and Merilee had left Camden the weekend before. Did Irene even know that Terence was a suspect in Clarkson's murder? "What were her other courses, Irene?"

"She has Reading. She's doing that for the second time. And Sociology. Do you know this teacher, Hargrave?"

"Yes. We've talked about Merilee. I told you before that her reading and writing skills are very low. My course and the Reading and Math are high school level to catch them up for college level work. Sociology is college level, and not being able to read well hurts her there. Irene, she can't read the questions on the tests."

"Why would they put her in Sociology then?"

"I don't know."

"I think she'd do better if she dropped sociology and worked on catching up. The deadline for dropping courses is March 22, next Wednesday."

"How many hours is she carrying?"

"Twelve, but that's too many for her."

"Irene, freshmen have to have at least twelve hours to stay in the dorm, and all of her courses are requirements."

"But we have to do something to get her off this academic probation."

Penny was thinking how there was nothing to do, but she didn't want to say that. She remembered that Oscar had already told the mother that Merilee shouldn't be in college. Now she said, "Why don't you call Dr. Farrell again. If anyone can help, he can. It's difficult, Irene. I'm not sure what to tell you. Let me ask you about something else. Do you know that the student who gave Merilee a ride back to college, Terence Jackson, is being held in jail here on suspicion of murder?"

"No. Oh, my lord. Why? He seemed such a nice young man. Who got killed?"

"The History professor Merilee had last semester, Dr. Clarkson. Terence may not have done it, but they have some evidence that makes them suspect him. Didn't any of the police down here call you?"

"I have a message from a Mr. Hargrave. I thought that was the sociology teacher, and I wanted to talk to you first. I've been gone all week. My mother took sick, and I've been helping her. Merilee went back to college Saturday evening, and I've been in Philadelphia until this morning seeing about Mama."

"Merilee left Camden Saturday evening?"

"Oh, yes. Terence and Ronny picked her up after dinner. They were going to drive all night, get back Sunday. I told her not to miss any more classes. She said you were angry that she missed that Thursday before break."

"Not angry. I was dismayed, and I told her she couldn't afford any more Fs. I have Ronny and Terence, too. They also should have been in class."

Penny was thinking, so they were back Sunday. Terence could have killed Clarkson, which was what the Raleigh police believed.

"You're sure they left Saturday evening?"

"Oh, yes, right on four o'clock. Mama called me just as it was getting dark, before six, I'm sure, and I drove over to Philly that night."

"Merilee, Ronny and Terence are claiming they left Sunday evening, got back here Monday morning."

"No, that can't be right." Then she stopped abruptly. "When was that professor killed?"

"He was found Monday morning, but they think it happened Sunday night."

"Now, if Merilee says they left here Sunday evening, they did. I'll have to talk to her. She didn't have no permission to hang around Camden with Terence and Ronny. She don't lie, Miz Weaver. If she says she left Sunday evening, then they must have went back Sunday evening."

~

It was Tuesday afternoon before Penny saw Merilee. She hadn't been in class that morning, nor had she come to Penny's office hours, but Oscar had dropped by a little before twelve to ask her to join him in his office at two to talk to Merilee. "I told the Dean that her mother was worried about her grades, and we were, too, since she hasn't been coming to class, so she's bringing her at two. The Dean won't stay, but she'll make sure Merilee comes over."

When Penny arrived at two, Merilee was crying. Oscar had seated her in his own comfortable swivel chair and had taken a nearby straight chair. Merilee buried her head in her hands when Penny walked in. Oscar gestured Penny to a chair and said, "Merilee, we're here to help you. We know you're worried about your grades. Let's talk everything over and see what we can work out."

He spoke gently. She lifted her head, tears still streaming. He handed her a clean handkerchief, another neatly ironed and folded one, from his pocket, and waited.

"Miz Weaver mad wid me on account of I didn't go to class."

"I'm not angry, Merilee, but Dr. Ferrell and I are worried about you because you've missed two weeks of class, before break, all last week and now this morning."

Oscar held up his hand. "Merilee, please tell us what's making you cry."

She wiped her eyes and blew her nose, then said, her voice catching, "I can't have no baby."

Penny was startled. It was true, and Merilee apparently knew. Oscar glanced at Penny. She hadn't told him that Merilee had had her tubes tied.

"You're young now. Having a baby can wait," he said. "Right now you're in college. How are you feeling about that?"

"I want me a white baby. Some of them girls in Camden done got white babies."

Oscar looked bowled over, but he plunged on. "Do you think a white-skinned baby is better than a brown-skinned baby, Merilee?" He looked at Penny like he couldn't believe where this conversation was going. He's game, Penny thought. He's trying to find out about Merilee's feelings, and they're coming out.

"White babies are better," she said. She sounded defiant, sure of her ground, and stopped crying.

Oscar shook his head, incredulous. "Merilee, that's not true." He got up and paced between where Merilee was sitting and where Penny was. Only about eight feet, not much room for pacing. "I'm very dark-skinned. You have much lighter skin that I do, but skin color has nothing to do with what makes people better or worse. We're all different, and we can be good at different things. Mrs. Weaver and I are good at teaching English. You're good at singing, Merilee. I heard you sing at the Black History Convocation. Your voice is really beautiful, Merilee."

Penny said quietly, "I agree."

"I like to sing," said Merilee, "but Mama want me to get my education first. She don't want me to have no baby. She done made me do that operation so I can't have no baby, and I want one. I want me a white baby." Then she smiled sweetly at Penny. Oscar looked so anguished when he sat down, it was as if he couldn't stand up.

Merilee continued: "Mama say, 'Drop one class.' I do bad in all my classes now. I don't know which of them to drop. Mama say I have to by tomorrow."

"Merilee," said Oscar, still gently. Penny thought *he* was going to cry. "You can't drop any of your courses. You have twelve credit hours, and you need all those hours to stay in college. Your mother called me, and I told her. You can't drop any of the courses you're taking and stay here at the college."

Penny surprised herself when she spoke next. "Merilee, if you'll go to all your classes, not miss any more, I'll tutor you in reading and composition. I think they have a good math tutor, too, don't they, Dr. Farrell?"

Oscar shook his head in dismay. Penny shrugged. They both knew it was unlikely anything could help Merilee. Why did Penny want to try? Because she hated it when the odds were so stacked? It made her rebel. At least they'd know better if Merilee definitely shouldn't be in college. Penny was encountering for the first time the inside Merilee. Oscar was pulling that out. Merilee deserved her chance. Penny could read Oscar's skepticism in his face and his despair in the way his shoulders slumped. Then he roused himself.

"Merilee, Ms. Weaver has offered to help you, but you must promise me and her to attend every single class you have and every tutoring session she schedules. Will you do that? You understand that right now your grades are much too low. You must do better to stay here at St. Francis."

Merilee had stopped crying. She handed his handkerchief back to Oscar and stood up. "Thank you, Dr.

Ferrell. Thank you, Miz Weaver. I want to stay here. I be in class now, Miz Weaver. Ima go back to my room now."

"Promise me, Merilee, you'll go to all your classes and all your tutoring sessions with Ms. Weaver?" pressed Oscar. "When will the first session be, Ms. Weaver?"

"Can you meet at nine-fifteen, right after our class, Merilee, starting this coming Thursday?"

"Yes, ma'am."

She walked toward the door. Oscar stood. She turned. "Yes, sir. I'll go to class to Ms. Weaver." She turned back to the door. Then he unlocked and opened his office door, and she walked slowly out, calm again, as if nothing had ever upset her.

Oscar watched until she turned toward the elevator and then shook his head and looked at Penny. "It's hopeless," he whispered.

Thursday morning Ronny Glover scooted in just as she was closing and locking the classroom door at ten minutes past eight, but no Merilee. Ronny looked around. His favorite seat by the back window had been usurped by the football player named Larry. Ronny sat down in the front row right in front of Penny, in Terence's seat.

On Tuesday she had given them a short selection from Zora Neale Hurston's chapter in her autobiography called *The Inside Search*. She was asking them to write a five-paragraph essay treating the visions Hurston had had as a problem. Then they were to tell what their solution would be or how they would handle it if they'd seen her twelve scenes like "clear-cut stereopticon slides," or they could give a similar vision experience they'd had and how they had solved living with it. They couldn't ignore the vision, either Hurston's or their own. They needed to think up a way to deal with it, make it part of their lives.

They would work on their drafts in class, and she'd be there to advise, answer questions. The other students had gone to work when Ronny arrived. Penny handed him the copy of Hurston's vision and her guidelines for their essay.

He looked baffled. "Is this what we be doing today?" He glanced around at the others, heads bent, writing away. She nodded. "I'm sorry I missed so much class, Miz Weaver. I was worried about my boy Terence. He still in that jail. He tole me: 'Go to class. Miz Weaver will help you.' I want to make up my work. I don't want no F. Coach say I can't play no football next season if'n I got Fs."

Penny thought about the mentally challenging assignment she'd given him. He probably couldn't read the Hurston passage or the suggestions for writing the essay. He was apparently the only one, as the rest were writing or staring into space thinking. She certainly had a penchant for taking on hopeless tasks, first Merilee, now Ronny.

She pulled over her chair and began explaining to him what he needed to do. He listened but seemed restive, distracted. "Where Merilee?"

"She's not here today. If you see her, tell her to call me. She's behind in her work, too. I'll give you until next Tuesday to catch up, Ronny, but right now I want you to outline your essay. Now do you want to write about Zora Neale Hurston's vision of what her life would be like or your own?"

"What a vision?"

"It's when you see ahead of time what your life could be like. You imagine or you dream of how it will be in the future."

"Like me being an NFL player?"

"Yes, or when you told me you wanted to walk across the stage and get your degree."

"Oh, yeah. Okay. Ima write about that."

She told him what should go in the first paragraph and returned to her desk, where another student was waiting.

She'd helped three or four, approved several opening paragraphs and made suggestions here and there. Generally, she was pleased. Not only Sheila and Lashandra, but they all seemed engaged, their minds working on the assignment, interested, not bored. Finally she was connecting with them.

Then she looked over at Ronny and saw that his notebook was there, but he was not. Lashandra was sitting next to him. She looked up, saw Penny looking at Ronny's chair, and gestured to the door. Penny walked over, opened it, and looked toward the elevator, then the other way, toward the men's room. No Ronny. Then he walked out of the men's room. He was talking on his cell phone. She had forbidden their phones being on in class, receiving or making calls. Now it occurred to her that going to the bathroom, which she now permitted, though they were supposed to ask, was perfect cover for cell phone calls. She almost said something. Then she heard what he was saying. "Don't tell nobody nothin' 'bout that night, Merilee. Terence in jail over one murder. You want him to fry for two murders? Forget that night like it never happened. That broad was stupid anyway. She better off dead. You want them to put us in jail, too? Nah, I gotta go.

Miz Weaver be mad." He shut off his phone. He'd turned away to finish his conversation.

Penny was thinking, so he and Merilee were at Audrey White's house the night she died. Had Terence killed her then? Were Ronny and Merilee were witnesses? She set her thoughts aside when he turned. She beckoned him to her.

"Ronny, you do not use your cell phone during class time. You have only half an hour now to finish drafting your essay. I'll keep your phone until class is over. I'm not very impressed, Ronny. You have a lot of catching up to do. Now get to work."

He put the phone in his pocket. "I'll work, Miz Weaver. You ain't seen me really work, but I promise I will now." She held out her hand and stood in front of the door. Finally he gave the phone to her.

"It's turned off?"

"Yes, ma'am."

She opened the door. "Now get to work. Impress me, Ronny."

The ritual of discipline, of classroom order, of scolding him and confiscating his phone helped keep her mind from the loud interior voice she was hearing: one of your students is a murderer.

Later, she told her mind. I'll call Derek later. Best now to keep things normal. She didn't think Ronny realized she'd heard what he'd said on his cell phone to Merilee. She hoped not.

He did seem subdued as he fitted himself back into his chair and looked at the page closely covered with writing that was in front of Lashandra. Then he opened his notebook and began writing.

Penny was across the room checking another student's

essay when he raised his hand. "Miz Weaver, how you spell *certificate*?"

Seventeen

Thursday, March 22. Penny had explained before Ronny arrived that she wanted to collect all their drafts. She would grade each draft. Next Tuesday she'd give these back, and they could revise and do a second draft in class and get an additional grade.

She gave Ronny back his phone and collected his paper. He had written four lines. Most of the students had covered a whole page. She wondered if she should ask him to come with her to Oscar's office, but it seemed wiser to let him go as she normally would and go consult Oscar herself. They could call Derek, whose cell and beeper numbers she had. She had planned to be tutoring Merilee after this class, but no Merilee. That plan had fallen to the ground. Merilee was somehow involved, too. Penny needed a sane head to help her sort this one out.

Oscar was always in his office at nine-fifteen. She suspected him of being there in case she came by for her mail or to say hello, but he wasn't there today. In her mailbox she found a memo about the Good Friday holiday, April 13. She'd wait a few minutes. His door was open, so he'd probably be right back. She settled into the chair where his secretary would sit if he had a secretary and pulled out the class papers she had collected. She read Ronny's first.

"I been wanten to play NFL ball sense I be 8 yers old. Now I be in collag. It my chance. I bees good in school. I score more than any buddy in my school my last year." That was as far as he'd gotten. Not bad for Ronny. She wondered if he'd finish this essay, much less make it to the NFL.

Oscar walked right past her into his office. She stepped over to his door.

"Penny. I didn't see you. I thought you were tutoring Merilee in the Writing Center."

"I'd planned to, Oscar. She wasn't in class, but there's worse news."

He gestured to the chair where she always sat and shut the door after her. "That's bad enough. It was brave of you to try, but I don't think she can benefit from tutoring. Something is too terribly wrong."

How to break it to him that things were wrong beyond what they'd imagined? They hadn't exactly thought Terence innocent, but they'd had no idea two comparative innocents had been caught up in whatever he was doing at Audrey White's house. They hadn't even known for sure that Terence had been there. She sat down. "It's pretty bad. Ronny finally came back to class. I do let them take bathroom breaks now. Anyway, he disappeared, and I found him talking on his cell phone in the hall."

"Oh, cell phones. I'd like to smash every one of them. Can't afford text books, but they all have fancy cell phones."

"It's not that, Oscar. It's what I heard Ronny saying. I'm pretty sure he was talking to Merilee about Audrey's murder. They were both there, and Terence, too, that

night. Ronny called Audrey a dumb broad and said she
was better off dead.

~

Penny had seldom been so glad to see Derek as when
he was waiting in the hall at the end of her Creative
Writing seminar that Thursday. He didn't come into the
classroom until all the students but Obie had filed out. He
nodded to Obie.

"Thank God you're here, Derek," she said, zipping her
back pack.

Obie hesitated.

"It's okay, Obie. You can go." She'd seen his worried
look. Then it occurred to her that he would know where
Ronny was. "No, wait, please. You may be able to tell us
where Ronny Glover would be now. Derek, hold on a
minute."

"Ronny?" Obie looked at his watch. "We have a team
meeting at twelve-thirty. He's probably in the cafeteria or
in his room in Simon Green dorm, that's next to the
library. You need me to find him or go with you?" He
looked from Derek to Penny.

"Maybe. Derek, I think you need to talk to Ronny.
From something I heard him say, I think he has
information you need."

She didn't want to go into details in front of Obie, but
Derek said, "Gotcha. Obie, I would appreciate it if you'd
help me find him. Penny, can you wait in Oscar's office? I
hope we'll be right back. Tell Oscar I'd appreciate him
waiting, too."

Penny said, "Of course. I'll go there now. I talked with Oscar two hours ago. He knew I'd asked you to come."

Twenty minutes later Ronny appeared with Derek. Oscar got up and suggested Ronny sit in his swivel chair. Given his size and balloon arms, it was the most comfortable, but at this moment for Ronny it was the hot seat. He looked suspiciously at the chair. "I ain't done nothin'," he said, but he sank into Oscar's chair.

Derek sat down on the straight chair nearest Ronny, and Oscar sat right by the door after he'd locked it. Penny had shifted to the chair on Oscar's left beside the one where she usually sat.

Derek put a tape recorder on the desk near Ronny. "I'd like to hear your story, Ronny. You're not under arrest, but I want your statement. I'll get it typed, and then we'll get you to sign it. You know that I'm with the Shagbark County Sheriff's Department and in charge of investigating the death of Ms. Audrey White, who was Provost here?"

"I ain't done nothin'."

"Give me your full name and address, Ronny, here at school and at home."

He did, shaking his head, his dreads looking messy. When he glanced at Penny, he looked terrified. She thought he might cry, this huge, bloated man. Inside somewhere for all his bluster he was still a very little boy.

"Where were you on the night of February 14, a Wednesday, Ronny?"

"I don't know. I ain't been anywhere."

"Do you know Terence Jackson, Ronny?"

"Yeah. He my boy. We from Camden."

"Did you ride to Camden with Terence for spring break, Ronny?"

"None o' yore bidness."

Oscar said, "Ronny, you'll help yourself more by answering the lieutenant's questions."

"Yeah, I went home for break. Terence give me a ride, else I ain't able to go home. They ain't give us our money."

"What day did you leave for spring break, Ronny?"

"I ain't remember."

"Ms. Weaver, did you understand that Ronny and Merilee Taylor were riding home to Camden with Terence Jackson?"

"Yes. Merilee told me the Tuesday before that they were leaving that day. That would have been February 27. The break was from March 3 to 11, but many students left early that week."

"Ronny, did you leave that day, Tuesday, February 27, for the car ride to Camden with Terence?"

"Maybe."

Derek was being infinitely patient. "Did you go to your Wednesday, Thursday or Friday classes the week before break?"

"No, sir. Terence, his boy was kilt. He had to leave early, and Merilee and me, we ain't had no ride and no money to catch the bus."

"So you left that Tuesday, February 27?"

"Yes, sir."

"When did you return from Camden after spring break, Ronny?"

This time he was eager to answer. "We got back Monday morning right about eight o'clock. We had us some breakfast at the Hardee's out on the highway.

Terence and me, we drove all night. Merilee, she slept. She went to her classes. Terence and me, we too tired. We sleep till lunch."

Penny was sure now that he was lying about the day of their return. Derek looked serene, unworried. Ronny was sitting up straight now, no longer scared.

"Let's think back, Ronny, to the week before you left early for spring break. That was the week Ms. Weaver began teaching your class. Her first day teaching was Tuesday, February 13. The next day was Wednesday. What did you do the next day, that Wednesday?"

"I ain't remember."

Derek turned off the tape. Ronny started to get up, but Derek motioned him to sit back down. Oscar, beside Penny, was tense, as if he expected to fight with Ronny. Derek said casually, "Only one more question, Ronny, for now. I understand you and Merilee were with Terence at the Provost's house, Mrs. White, the night she was killed. Did Terence take her some cocaine? Was that why you and Merilee were there?"

"We ain't." Ronny turned red in the face and jumped up again. Oscar leapt to his feet, too.

"We ain't," Ronny said louder. "Merilee and me, we ain't done nothin'."

"Nothing? I have a witness that you beat and then killed Professor Clarkson the Sunday evening of the last day of spring break."

"It weren't my doo-rag," shouted Ronny and lunged for the door. Oscar jumped in front of the door, but Derek moved faster. He pulled Ronny around, his hands behind his back, pulled out handcuffs, cuffed him, and forced him to sit back down. "I'm arresting you, Ronny Glover. You're a suspect in the murders of Audrey White and Edmund Clarkson. Anything you say may be used against you in a court of law. You have the right to remain silent. You may retain a lawyer. Ronny, I'm taking you to the Raleigh Police Station now. Come along quietly. It will go better for you." He spoke kindly. Ronny hung his head down. He was bigger than Derek, but Derek was wiry and fit, as was Oscar, standing in front of Penny now as if to protect her.

Derek pulled out his cell phone and punched in a number. "We're coming out. Meet us in the outer English Department office, and clear the hallways on the fourth floor first, park the elevator, and station some of your guards at the stairways. Right."

He turned to Penny and Oscar. "Oscar, could you step back with Penny." The open door revealed two uniformed Raleigh police and two security guards behind them, one being Rosa. Ronny was escorted away by the uniformed men, Derek following. The security guards had gone on ahead to clear the halls.

"Why is Derek so sure he was involved in both murders?" Oscar asked after he'd shut the outside departmental door.

"I don't know that he's sure," said Penny. She was fairly certain that Derek had lied about the witness to get Ronny to confess. She went over and sat down. She was shivering, scared afterwards. That had happened to her before. "Ronny definitely knows something. Do you think he did it?"

"I don't know what to think," said Oscar. "These poor kids. It seems Merilee's somehow mixed up in this, too? None of them have any business being in college."

~

Penny called Kenneth as soon as she had a chance. Oscar said she could use his phone because he had a meeting with the Provost. "He may be firing me," he said as he walked quickly away.

Kenneth was upset that she had been so close to the new suspect, maybe the killer.

"We don't know for sure yet, Kenneth, but he apparently knows something about both murders."

"I don't like it, love."

"I didn't figure you would."

"Where are you now?"

"In Oscar's office. I'll be fine. Terence and Ronny are in jail. Oscar will be back about one o'clock. I'll eat my lunch here and then go over to the library. I'm still shook up, but I'll be fine. I hate it that Ronny and Merilee got caught up in whatever Terence did. It's all pretty confusing, but Derek will figure it out."

"Not soon enough for me. Listen, I'm coming to work early. If you'll please stay where you are, I can be there by one. I'm putting on my uniform right now."

"Okay, I'll wait here. I'll be fine, Kenneth, really. I'm sad but not scared."

"Sit tight," he said and hung up.

At twelve-thirty Merilee strolled into the English Department office and saw Penny sitting at the secretary's desk.

"Miz Weaver, I was looking for Dr. Farrell. I'm sorry I missed my tutoring. I has my period, and I been so sick, too sick to get to class this morning."

She looked pasty and exhausted. What should Penny do? Merilee had already broken her promise. Oscar would say she'd lost her chance. He'd tell Penny again that it was hopeless. Merilee did not have the brain she needed to learn.

Penny wasn't sure afterwards why she said, "If I excused you, would you be free now to do the tutoring? I brought a different book that might help you, and I prepared some exercises for you. Shall we try them?"

"Yes, ma'am." She had tears in her eyes. "Will Dr. Ferrell be mad wid me?"

"I don't know, Merilee. He's not here right now. We can talk to him when he gets back. You're free?"

"Yes, ma'am." More tears.

"Come sit here, Merilee. Don't cry. We'll work in here. I can shut this outer office door. Nobody will bother us."

Penny got up and took the plastic clock sign that hung on Oscar's door and pointed it to his return time at one o'clock, hung it on the outer office door and locked it.

"Okay, let's see what we can do. We're working on a new essay now. This book shows you the main parts or paragraphs of a problem/solution essay. See here, in the first paragraph, you write down the problem. Then in the second paragraph you describe the problem in more detail, maybe why you want to solve it. Then in the third paragraph you write down a possible solution. In the fourth you tell how you could carry it out, how the solution could actually work. In the last paragraph you write your conclusion."

As she talked Penny was thinking of all Merilee's problems and how there weren't any easy solutions, at least that she could see. But if Merilee were living at home and singing in her church choir and were loved, her singing voice valued, maybe some of this awfulness that was around her here would be eased, would disappear. Maybe, hopefully, her mother would have learned something.

"Yes, ma'am." They both studied the diagram of the essay. Then Penny explained about having a dream or vision as the problem, and slowly she drew out from Merilee that she wanted to be a singer like Mahalia Jackson, famous for that song Merilee had sung at the convocation: "He's Got the Whole World in His Hands."

Penny said that was a good start. She did have a beautiful voice, and she sang that song so very well. In Merilee's own words Penny helped her write her dream down and explained that a dream became a problem because it didn't simply happen. You had to work toward it. You couldn't get there if you forgot about it or pushed it away.

It was nearly one by the time they'd worked through the second paragraph. Merilee wanted to be a singer, but her mother said she had to go to college to get there, and she was doing terrible in her classes, and now Terence was in jail. Her boyfriend Ronny, too. She was crying again. So she'd heard. Of course, students must have seen Ronny being taken away by the police. Someone had told her.

"Are you worried about Terence and Ronny?"

"Yes, ma'am."

"The police are trying to learn the truth, what really happened when Mrs. White and Dr. Clarkson died."

"They was bad," Merilee said fiercely. "They was mean to me. They was better off dead." Then she burst into tears again.

Penny had a sudden intuition that she didn't want to believe, but she knew the ones that zinged in without warning were usually right. She glanced at her watch. Oscar or Kenneth would be here any minute. What should she do?

Then Merilee solved it. "Oh, Miz Weaver, I didn't mean to make them dead. I didn't know they be dead." She was sobbing now brokenheartedly. Penny moved her chair closer and put her arms around her. What a confusing world she lived in. Poor baby, she thought.

Someone knocked at the door. "Penny?" It was Oscar.

She said to Merilee, "It's Dr. Farrell. I'll let him in."

She walked over and opened the door. Oscar looked worried; then he saw Merilee. Penny put her finger on her lips. "Listen first, Oscar, before you say anything. Merilee's very sad."

Merilee looked up at him. He'd put a kindly expression on his face. He could be so gentle with these children. That's what they were, children.

"What's wrong, Merilee?"

She sobbed, and Penny sat down again and held her.

"Tell me, Merilee. We can't help you if you don't tell us."

"That lady ..."

"Yes?" encouraged Oscar.

"Mrs. White?" asked Penny.

"Yes, ma'am. Terence took me and Ronny to her big house on account of she wanted crack from Terence. He give it to her, and she said sit down. We wanted to leave. She wanted us to say how big and nice her house was. 'Merilee, wouldn't you like to have this big house?' she say.

"I say, 'Yes, ma'am.' She were drunk. She couldn't hardly walk. She say, 'Here, Merilee, see my bedroom. See, Merilee, if you smart like me, you can get you a big house. See the nice king-size bed?'

"Then she fell down on the bed. I were scared. I thought she were dead. She were lying there with her eyes shut. But I ain't smart. I ain't never gonna have no big house, no king-size pretty bed. I don't know why I touched her. She were mean to me. I just pushed on her neck to see were she dead.

"When Terence came in, he say, 'Stop Merilee, you done kilt her. We gotta leave here fast. C'mon.' So we did. He tol' Ronny and me never say nothin', say weren't none of us over to her house. But the police got Terence and Ronny. They gonna get me, too, 'cause them boys didn't kill Miz White or Dr. Clarkson. I did. I never mean to, but Terence, he say I kilt the both on them."

Eighteen

Thursday, March 22. When Kenneth arrived shortly after one, Oscar and Penny were both crying. Penny was holding Merilee. Oscar stood when Kenneth came in. He reached in his pocket for his handkerchief, forgetting he'd given it to Merilee. Penny handed him a tissue box from the secretary's desk.

"You all okay?" Kenneth asked quietly.

Penny knew in that moment more than she had ever known before that it was Kenneth's arms and only his that she wanted around her. She stood up and walked into them, and Oscar sat down next to Merilee and put his arms around her. Penny heard him saying, "I'll help you through this, Merilee. I'll do everything in my power."

To Kenneth Penny whispered, "I love you so much. Merilee killed them. Get Derek."

Kenneth held her away so he could see her eyes. He didn't believe her. She nodded.

"Wait here," he said. "I'll call him and then stay with you until he gets here." And he did.

The rest of the day Penny was hardly aware of what happened. Sammie turned up after Derek had taken Merilee away, again accompanied by Raleigh police. Oscar insisted on going with them. Kenneth had called Kate, who would meet them at the jail.

Sammie coaxed Penny to talk on the drive home, but after she told the bare bones, all she could say or think was, "It's so sad, so wrong."

Sammie insisted on staying with her, made her some scrambled eggs, toast, tea, and was silent or listened whenever Penny felt like talking. She didn't much. She was stunned, exhausted, but wide awake. Sammie was making them Ovaltine when Kenneth got back at eleven-thirty. Derek was with him.

Sammie got out more milk to make more Ovaltine, and Derek gave Penny a hug. "You did it again, Penny. You solved my case and the Raleigh case, too. Merilee didn't intend to kill White. I think she was trying to feel her pulse, but she pressed on the carotid artery and killed her. Then they all got scared and left.

"Now we know that the three of them did come back early from Camden, got here Sunday morning, arranged for Merilee to meet Clarkson in his office. The boys wanted to get him back for his treatment of Merilee. They used her as bait. He fell right into the trap. She let in the boys when his pants were down, and they beat him up. Then they egged her on to kill him using Terence's doo-rag. It all came out finally. Whew, what a hard one."

"What will happen to Merilee?" asked Sammie.

"Kate was there. She's representing them all. For now Merilee will be in Women's Prison, also in Raleigh."

"But what will happen to her after the trial?" asked Penny. "Life imprisonment? It's so sad." She knew she sounded like a broken record, but she couldn't help it.

"Kate thinks in a mental hospital but probably for life. Butner, unless her parents can afford a better situation."

"That beautiful voice," said Penny.

"Kate said to tell you she sees what you see in Merilee. Penny, she'll do everything she can. It will go harder on Terence and Ronny. They egged her on. I hold them responsible, but we'll see what the D.A. goes for. I'm sorry, Penny. You and Oscar were great with her. He stayed right with her all day, Penny, and her mother's coming in tomorrow. She'll be able to visit her.

"Oh, and Oscar said to tell you the new Provost did fire him, right before he came back and found you and Merilee crying, but he said it's the least of his worries now."

The next morning Penny slept late. When she woke, Kenneth was gone, and the sun was streaming through the window that faced toward the garden the way it did mid-morning. Ten already. She worked her feet into slippers, pulled on her robe and walked over to the window. She could see Andy and Kenneth standing near the fence between the garden and the orchard.

The grape vines were black. Oh, no. The frost they'd worried about had happened. She ran down the stairs and turned toward the orchard. The peach and apple blossoms were brown. The new tender leaves on the big oak tree that shaded Belle's house had withered.

Then she saw Belle's daffodils. They had frost on them as the grass did where it was still in the shade, but as the sun touched them, the frost was melting, and the daffodils looked as bright and fresh as they had the day before. The frost hadn't gotten everything, but too much. A killer frost.

~

Penny and Kenneth were back in their apartment, drinking coffee, when Sarah drove in. Kenneth got up to look. "She's got Seb with her." Penny thought how much brighter Seb's future looked than Merilee's had ever had a chance to look, even if his parents were struggling. He was like a cheerful daffodil himself. "Happy Seb," he babbled, and "Toast. Seb want toast."

Kenneth sat him on a chair with the Raleigh phone book under him and supplied him toast and juice, and Sarah with a cup of coffee. "You're off work today?" he asked.

"No, I have to go back. Mom, I know this is late notice."

Penny laughed. "You want me to keep Seb, right?"

"Would you?"

"Yes. All day?"

"Until I get off work? I can get back here by five, and Leroy will be here then. I want to tell him he can see Seb as much as he wants. Brian … well, Brian would like to see less of Seb, a lot less. Oh, Mom, what am I going to do?"

Penny laughed again. "Leave Seb. Come back and stay for supper. Talk to Leroy. He'll be happy. Seb's happy. I'm happy. We have daffodils."

Sarah looked baffled.

Penny thought, I'm not simply happy. I'm sad, too. But maybe He does have Seb in his hands, and Sarah, and even Merilee, Ronny, and Terence. Frost happens, but so do daffodils.

Meet Author Judy Hogan

Judy Hogan founded Carolina Wren Press (1976-91), and was co-editor of *Hyperion Poetry Journal* from 1970 to 1981. She has published five volumes of poetry and two prose works with small presses. She has taught all forms of creative writing since 1974.

Judy joined Sisters in Crime in 2007 and has focused on writing and publishing eight traditional mystery novels. In 2011 she was a finalist in the St. Martin's Malice Domestic Mystery contest. The twists and turns of her life's path over the years have given her plenty to write about. She is also a small farmer and lives in Moncure, North Carolina.

CPSIA information can be obtained at www.ICGtesting.com
Printed in the USA
BVOW030733020312

284265BV00001B/1/P